Deepwater

"There's nothing else to be done!" he roared at Mother and me across the kitchen table that evening. "I can't manage the farm on my own. Char must leave school. She'll have to help me! . . . High School be damned! The war's put an end to all that! If the girl's got any brains, she can use them on the farm. The boy's deserted us. The girl will have to pay for it!"

Also available in Magnet

Stringybark Summer

JUDITH O'NEILL

Deepwater

A Magnet Book

To the memory of
Isobel Keith, Phyllis Rowntree
and Katharine Collinson

First published in Great Britain
by Hamish Hamilton Children's Books 1987
This edition first published in 1989
by Magnet Paperbacks
Michelin House, 81 Fulham Road, London SW3 6RB
Copyright © 1987 Judith O'Neill
Printed in Great Britain
by Cox & Wyman Ltd, Reading

ISBN 0 416 12642 1

Contents

1. Shifting the School

When the war started — the Great War as we used to call it — my brother Laurie was the first in our valley to join up. Plenty of boys went into the army after him but he was the first. I think he was glad to get away. The valley can seem like a prison if you've never once been out of it. That war gave Laurie his chance. He just left the cows one Monday morning after the milking and went. He got to Egypt and Gallipoli and France and all sorts of foreign places over there. He was in hospital in England for a while too. And at the end of it all, he came safely home again. He was one of the lucky ones.

The day that Laurie left, Mother was crying and Dad was angry. They were proud of him in a way — rushing off like that on the spur of the moment to defend the Empire — but they didn't want to lose him. Dad was angry from fear. He was scared that Laurie might be killed. And he was angry because of the farm. He couldn't possibly run it single-handed. It was far too much for one man alone. Laurie had been working with Dad for well over four years, ever since Grandpa had died. They'd done everything together and the farm was in good shape. That was the year when the drought really began to bite. It had started up slowly in 1913 — so slowly that we hardly noticed it at first. We certainly didn't worry in the first few months. We were sure there'd be rain tomorrow. But by the middle of 1914, everyone in the valley was worried. In June and July, when we usually expected a decent winter downpour, hardly a drop had fallen. The paddocks were beginning to look brown and the sheep seemed a bit skinny. The little creek that ran down through our farm from the ridge to the river was shrinking at the edges. We had

1

no idea then just how much worse it was going to be but already Dad was beginning to wonder if the new crops would grow at all — the wheat and the oats. August was just as bad as June and July and it was at the very end of August that Laurie walked off. Dad was afraid the whole farm would fall to pieces — with Laurie gone and no sign of rain. Where could he find another man to help him? They were all going off to the war. How could he pay for one, even if he found one? The farm was hardly going to support our family that year, let alone a permanent man as well. No wonder he was angry. I remember the day still with Mother sobbing and Dad shouting.

That's when Dad thought of me. I was just fourteen then and in my last year at the little school at Kanyul. I'd been hoping to go on to the High School in Wallaceville the next year. That was our nearest town, twenty miles off, and I would've had to board with another family there but I didn't mind that idea at all. In fact I was looking forward to it. Mother had always had great plans for my future. She said she didn't want me to end up as a farmer's wife in the valley. She even thought I might be a teacher or a nurse. Getting married was part of her plan for me, of course. Every girl had to get married. But not too young and not to a farmer in the valley. She liked the life well enough for herself. She'd grown used to it. But she wanted something different and better for me. Dad had always gone along with these ambitions of hers mildly enough up till that moment but he abandoned them all on the day that Laurie went off to the war.

"There's nothing else to be done!" he roared at Mother and me across the kitchen table that evening. "I can't manage this farm on my own. Char must leave school. She'll have to help me!"

I'm always called Char. Char as in Charlotte, not as in Charles.

"But she was going to the High School next year," protested Mother. "She was going to board with Mrs Russell and just come home for the weekends. It's all arranged. I've started to make the uniform, Alec."

"High School be damned! The war's put an end to all that. If the girl's got any brains, she can use them on the farm. The boy's deserted us. The girl will have to pay for it!"

Dad glared at me, waiting for my protest.

Oddly enough, I didn't protest. I felt sad about leaving school so suddenly like that, before the year had even ended, but I was strangely excited at the idea of being counted as a grown-up almost overnight. I'd be Dad's right-hand woman since he couldn't have a right-hand man. I loved the farm. And anyway, the war wouldn't last long — or so I thought. It'd all be over by Christmas. Then I could still go in to the High School as Mother had planned.

"All right," I said, "I'll leave."

Dad was so astonished to find he didn't have to fight a long drawn-out battle with me that for once he had nothing to say. He just rubbed one big hand slowly over his balding head. Mother put her face down on the red oil-cloth on the table and cried louder.

"It's only for a few months, Mother," I pleaded. "Then Laurie'll be back again. I don't mind. Really I don't."

"But I mind!" she said. "Farming's no life for a girl! It's filthy work! You'll turn into a weather-beaten old hag! And what will the neighbours say? It's fair enough for the women to lend a hand in busy times but to work on the farm every day like a man — it's just not right! There's not one other girl in this whole valley who'll have to slave away like that!"

In fact she was wrong about that, though we didn't know it back in 1914. The war made a difference. Before it was over there were girls working on lots of the farms. Down in the city there were even girls working in the factories — or so we heard.

I went to bed and left Mother and Dad to argue it out. Dad won, of course. He always did. The very next morning I started on the farm. I'd been helping with the milking for years anyway. All the kids in our valley had to do that. But from that day onwards I gradually took on all Laurie's old jobs as well — the lambing, the dipping, the hay-making and the chaff-cutting, the separating and the butter-churning, picking the walnuts and the apples, even killing off the rabbits that swarmed on the hill. The only thing Dad wouldn't let me do was the ploughing. He always did that himself with the two big horses pulling his plough.

Dad was a good teacher. Surprisingly patient.

"You do it this way, girl," he'd say as we tackled each new job and I'd try to make my hands do what his practised hands were doing. Soon I got the knack of things. We worked together well. My arms and back ached unbearably in the first few weeks but then they settled down. I must have toughened up.

The war lasted much longer than anyone had ever expected. Four years. Dad and I ran that farm right through to the end with only a few extra men to help us out at shearing time. Then Laurie came back at last. But when he did come back he was quite different from the boy who'd gone away. He was thin and his face was tired and bitter. He'd lost all his old interest in farming. He only stayed three months and then he drifted off again. But that's another story altogether. The story I want to tell is about our valley in the first year of the war. The year of the drought. Some strange things happened that year. The details are still sharp and clear in my mind although it was all so long ago. I want to get them down now before they fade.

Gillespie's Track ran the whole length of a rich river valley in the north-east corner of Victoria. That river flowed north to join another river and together they flowed still further north to the Murray. We were right at the top of Gillespie's Track — the very last farm in the valley. Beyond our fences the hills were too steep for farming and beyond those hills were the mountains. Purple in summer and capped with snow in winter. Gillespie's Track ended abruptly at our farm gate. There was some kind of narrow track on through the mountains but you couldn't take a cart or a buggy up there. A good horse might get you through but no one wanted to go that way. Our life-line was in the other direction — north along Gillespie's Track by the river into Wallaceville. Our sale-yards were there and our bank and our rail-head to the

4

south. That was the only track we knew. Some of the valleys had a railway line by then but all we had was Gillespie's Track.

I often used to wonder about Gillespie himself. No one in the valley could remember much about him. He'd been the first to forge a way through the thick bush back in the 1870s. He'd been the first to cut down the trees and to bring in his cattle and sheep. But he hadn't lasted long. He'd sold off his land to the Douglas family and pushed on to another part of the State. He was never heard of again but the road up our valley is still called Gillespie's Track so he's not quite forgotten. There's proper bitumen on the roadway now but it wasn't like that in 1914. It was just a rough dirt track, riddled with ruts and as hard as iron.

The farms were all strung out along the length of the Track on the western side of the river. Every few miles you'd come across a general store and perhaps a little weather-board church and a one-teacher school. 'Bush schools' we called them though most of the bush had been cleared by then. The little cluster of six farms at our top end was known as Deepwater. I liked that name. I still do. In a good year it suited the place too. The river ran fast and deep there, racing down from the melted snow on the mountains, a rushing torrent in late winter and early spring. Even in summer and autumn, when the river moved more slowly, it still lay deep and cool on the bend near our farm. Or it did till the year of the drought.

The other farming families at Deepwater in those days were the Craiks, the Morisons, the Douglases, the Logans and the Henschkes with their ten children. Too many children, Mother always said, shaking her plump head and wondering how Mrs Henschke had ever let it happen. Mrs Henschke was her closest friend and Ruth Henschke was mine but we were on good terms with all the families at Deepwater. Apart from the farmers there were the Pollocks at the general store. And then there was Mr Mallorie. He lived on his own, high on the ridge behind our farm, in the original log hut that his father had built in the early days when Gillespie was still in the valley.

Mr Mallorie had sold off his land to the Craiks by the time the war started. He was too old to farm it himself and he had no sons to follow him. No daughters either. He'd never even had a wife. But he liked to stay on in the old hut with its shingle of stringybark. That roof looked old-fashioned to me but he always said it kept the weather out all right. The rest of us had nice little weather-board houses by that time with proper sheets of iron on the roof. There was always a wide verandah across the front of our houses and sometimes the whole way round. The tank stood by the back door to catch any water that ran off the roof. Mr Mallorie had a good spring by his house so he'd dug a bit of a well and didn't have to worry about rain.

People said that old Mr Mallorie had money. Under his mattress, they said. But I didn't believe them. His clothes were torn and dirty and he never ate anything much except for corned beef out of tins and the occasional rabbit that he caught in his trap up on the hillside behind his hut. There was a pile of empty rusting tins in his backyard from all his meals of corned beef. He certainly didn't look as if he had any money. I'm not even sure if he had a mattress.

"I don't sleep too good, lass," he used to say to me when he met me out along the Track or if he dropped in at our place for a yarn with Dad. He often dropped in. His father had been a mate of Dad's father, right back in the days when the canvas tents were put up along our valley and before the bark huts were built. Mr Mallorie was a lot older than Dad but they got on well. Mother always gave him a decent feed when he dropped in. I think he came for that as much as for the yarn with Dad. It made a change from his corned beef.

The little school for all the kids at our end was four miles down the Track from Deepwater at Kanyul. That wasn't fair. There were only about five or six kids living at Kanyul. The farmers there hadn't done so well and some of them had moved on. But there were nineteen or twenty of us at our end and we all had to walk or ride those four miles to Kanyul every school day, summer and winter. So that's really why the school was moved and that's where my story begins — on the day they moved the Kanyul school, lock, stock, and barrel, four miles up the Track to our end of the valley at Deepwater. Mr Craik had given the plot of land — a nice piece of flat grassland near the general store, just between the Track and the river. Dad said it was good of him to give it. Land's never cheap. I only wished they'd thought of moving the school a few years earlier. The shift came too late to help me. It was only about a week after Dad had said I had to leave the school.

The day of the move was a bright spring morning in early September, still cold and sharp though the sun was well up in a clear blue sky. The wattles were coming out — the silver and the golden and the blackwood — and they made brilliant splashes of yellow in amongst the grey-green gum trees. There was no work done on any of the farms at our end of the valley that day — apart from the milking, of course. All the men and all the kids had come down early to help with the shifting. I'd never seen a whole building move before and I didn't really believe it could be done till I saw it with my own eyes. I'd ridden along to Kanyul on Star with Ruth sitting up behind me and her little brother, Fred, perched behind her, his arms firmly round her waist. All the other kids from Deepwater came flocking down the Track behind us, some on their horses and others on foot. Just about everyone was there. Even old Mr Mallorie. He was shuffling along slowly in his broken boots and hitching up his trouser-legs with both hands gripping them just above the knees.

"What's he doing that for, Char?" Fred asked me, laughing at the old man after we'd passed him. "Has he lost his braces or something?"

Fred was the eighth of the Henschke kids. He must've been about nine years old then. He was very fair like all the rest of them and his eyes were blue. The oldest boys in the family were already grown up and working with their father on the farm. Margaret, the eldest girl, helped in the house and in the garden and all the others (apart from the little ones, Harry and Tom) took their turn with the milking. I liked Fred Henschke. He was a bonzer kid. I wouldn't have minded having a younger brother like him. But I wasn't going to let him laugh at Mr Mallorie. I soon put a stop to that.

"There's nothing wrong with his braces," I said. "He's just a poor old bloke. Don't you laugh at him, Fred. You'll be like that yourself one day."

"Will I?" said Fred in astonishment. "What about you? Will you be like that too?"

I nodded.

"Everyone ends up like that. If they don't die young. Don't they, Ruth?"

Ruth hadn't been listening. Her mind was on something else.

"Do sit still, Fred," she said. He was wriggling around behind her, trying to look back at Mr Mallorie. Luckily we reached the school and Fred began to forget about the problems of old age and early death.

The little school sat squarely in the middle of its dusty playground. It looked so firm and solid that I didn't see how it was going to move. The neat weather-boards were painted white and the iron roof was green. There was a verandah along the front and a shelter shed right down the back where the children could eat their play-lunch on rainy days — when we had any rainy days. On one side of the school stood the usual round tank. It was completely empty that September. When you banged it, it gave out a hollow ring. Half-way along the other side was the brick chimney and the fireplace. That's how our one school room was heated in winter. The teacher always had his desk up close to the fire. He was warmer than anyone else. We used to hope he'd call us out the front to look at our work. Then we could stand near the fire for a while.

At the far end of the playground near the shelter-shed were the two small lavatories. 'Girls' and 'Boys' they were labelled. Inside there was nothing but a deep earth pit under a plain wooden seat. Not far from the sheds, in one corner of the yard, was the enclosure for the horses that some of the kids rode to school. On that morning it was full of the farmers' horses, munching hay from their hessian nose-bags. And along the back fence stood a straggly row of Scots pines, all leaning one

8

way in the wind. The pioneers had planted those trees forty years earlier when Dad was a boy at the school. They're still there today.

"How ever is the school going to squeeze through the gate, Char?" asked Fred when we'd tied Star to the railings with the other horses.

"It won't!" I laughed. "The men'll have to take the front fence down. You'd better tag along with the other kids now, Fred. There they are — running down the side. You'll be well out of the way there. Ruth and I have to give Dad a hand."

"The bullocks!" screeched Fred. "I can hear them coming, Char! Listen!" And he raced off to swing on the wire fence at the left-hand side of the playground where all the smaller children were swaying already.

I watched Dad. He'd taken charge of the men. Some of them — Ruth's father among them — were crawling right underneath the school between the joists, loosening the nails and screws that had held it firm on its foundations since the day it was built. Others were at work on the chimney outside and the fireplace inside, detaching them from the timber walls and knocking out the bricks one by one. There wasn't much of a chimney left at all by the time they'd finished. Just a heap of bricks and rubble. Dad caught sight of Mr Mallorie who was leaning up against the flag-pole out in front of the school. That's where we used to salute the flag every Monday morning. "I love God and my country. I honour the flag. I will serve the King and cheerfully obey my parents, teachers and the law." We said it with our hands on our hearts.

"That flag-pole'll be coming down in a minute, Keith!" Dad shouted across to Mr Mallorie. "Mac's bullocks are on their way now! You'd better go along the side there with the kids!"

Mr Mallorie grumbled darkly to himself. He turned round to Ruth and me.

"They're packing me off with all them blooming kids!" he muttered. "I come all this way down here to help them shift the school and they pack me off with the kids!"

I couldn't help smiling to myself at the idea of Mr Mallorie helping with the move but I clapped my hand over my mouth so he wouldn't see the smile. Once I'd got it under control, I hurried across to him. Ruth ran with me.

"The bullocks are just about here, Mr Mallorie," I said seriously. "Best to be out of the way. You know what Mac's bullocks are like. And he's got two other teams with him today as well. Dad was only thinking of your safety."

Mr Mallorie let go of the flag-pole and staggered across the playground to join the row of children by the fence. He didn't try to climb on the wire but he held firmly to a post with one hand. The other hand kept pulling at his trouser-legs.

"Where's your belt, Grandpa?" shouted Ken Douglas rudely, rocking on the wire.

"Shut up!" said Fred Henschke, turning on Ken.

"Is he your Grandpa, Ken?" asked Ellie Craik in surprise. "I didn't know you had one."

"Nope. I just call him that. He's not anyone's Grandpa," said Ken.

We could all hear the bullocks by now. They were coming nearer and nearer, bellowing their way along Gillespie's Track and spilling over onto the dry grass verges. The dust rose above them and hung in the air. Mac and his mates must've been driving those animals all through the night. (Mac and his mates were the bullockies — their job was to drive the bullocks). Perhaps they'd even camped somewhere by the river and made an early start in the morning. By the time Dad and the other men had pulled down the front fence and dug up the white flag-pole, I could clearly see the massive heads of the front bullocks less than half a mile away.

Out of the open door of the school, the Morison boys and the Douglases were carrying the long benches and the desks. Then they went back for the pictures from the walls and the teacher's table and chair. Jeff Logan had the geography globe and Donny Pollock ran out with the tray of inkwells.

"Let's help them, Char!" said Ruth and we ran up the school steps onto the verandah. Jim Morison had his arms wrapped right around a huge framed photograph of the school kids back in the 1880s. They did look funny in their old-fashioned smocks. Their faces seemed white and sad. Ruth and I took hold of one side of the frame and the three of us carried it together.

"Why don't you leave all this stuff inside, Jim?" asked Ruth. "You could give it a free ride to the new place."

"Too risky," said Jim. "The desks could slide around the floor and the pictures'd come tumbling off the walls. This old teacher looks a bit fierce, doesn't he?" and he nodded his head to the grim-faced teacher in the photograph. "Nothing like our Mr Edwards."

I agreed with him. Mr Edwards was nice. He didn't use his strap much.

"There's your Dad in this photo, Jim," I said, pointing to a solemn little boy in the front row. "And there's my Dad next to him and Ruth's Dad on the other side." Those poor little pale-faced kids in the photo were running all the farms now. Their faces were browned with years of sun.

Just at that moment, Dad's voice roared out to us.

"Char! Ruth! Leave those things to the boys! The bullocks are here! You get along to the fence now!"

I felt a bit indignant at being shunted off to the side fence with all the little kids and Mr Mallorie. But when I saw the sunshine glinting on the bullocks' sharp horns and the dust rising from their stamping hooves as they poured into the playground, I was only too glad to grab Ruth's hand and make a dash to safety. We could even smell the huge beasts by now. They stank. A hot sweaty animal smell — not the warm and milky smell of our own cows in the shed at night but something harsh and raw that caught me in the back of the throat. The noise of the shouting drivers and the bellowing bullocks was deafening as they surged across the yard towards the school.

By that time the men had inserted a series of jacks all the way round the building. They pumped together on the handles and lifted the entire school just an inch or two above its foundations. Every farmer for miles around must have lent a couple of jacks to help with the job. Then the men pushed three strong bogies (long, low trucks) in under the building and fixed sets of wheels onto them at the front and the back. Meanwhile the bullocks had all been turned round so they had their tails to the school. They were lined up in three long teams of ten. Thirty beasts altogether! I'd never seen so many all at once. Black and white and brindled. Just turning them round and getting them yoked up to the poles and the heavy chains that ran back to the bogies took an age. The bullockies, high on their horses, cracked their long hide whips across the bullocks' backs again and again. I hated to watch them so I closed my eyes but nothing could shut out the acrid smell or the noise of shouting, swearing and whip-lashing. The dust was up our nostrils.

This took the whole morning. Dad and Mac called a halt. Lunchtime. The mothers arrived down from the farms in their buggies and jinkers with packets of thick sandwiches and with hot tea in billies. Mac said it was no time to be feeding his bullocks. They wouldn't pull well on a full stomach. But he was glad for them to stand and rest and chew their cud. Their big heads hung down and their feet were quiet. Ruth and I sat with the older kids outside the fences and the younger ones climbed up onto the buggies to be nearer their mothers. Everyone was happily eating and drinking — the men with the men, the women with the women, the kids with the kids. It was as good as a Sunday School picnic.

I tried lots of sandwiches. Mother's were definitely the best. She put more meat and more pickle into hers. I could see the men making straight for her pile. That one was the first to be finished. Then everyone started on Mrs Craik's sandwiches and Mrs Henschke's and Mrs Douglas's and Mrs Morison's and Mrs Logan's. Mrs Pollock from the store had brought some too and so had the mothers from Kanyul.

I carried another billy of tea and a few more mugs across to Dad and his mates under the row of pines. They were talking about the war. The war and the drought. Most conversations came round to those two topics sooner or later.

"Any news of Laurie?" Mr Douglas was asking Dad as I poured the tea into the mugs.

Dad looked worried and screwed up his eyes against the sun. He pushed his hat right to the back of his head.

"We've had a letter, Frank. He's still in the training camp down south. I daresay he'll be sailing soon. We don't know where to. Could be Egypt, I reckon, but the wife says it'll be France."

"My Col's off to join up next week," said Mr Douglas proudly. "Maybe he and Laurie'll meet up over there somewhere. You never know."

"Martin's going too," put in Mr Henschke. "He can't wait to get into it. He's down in the city now. There's some kind of delay. We don't know what the trouble is but he'll soon sort it out."

The city. Melbourne. Two hundred miles south. I'd never been there and neither had Mother or Dad. I rather envied Col Douglas and Martin Henschke and our Laurie getting as far as Melbourne though I can't say I wanted to follow them to Egypt and France and the war. I'd never wanted to live in a city. It must feel terribly cramped, I thought. But I'd have loved to go and have a look. Just a look.

"I've been counting up the days when we had any rain last month," said Dad. "Three! And only a drop on each of them. Usually we can expect at least twelve days' rain at this time of the year — and good soaking rain at that."

"Don't worry, Alec," said Mr Morison. He always took a cheerful view of things. "This dry spell'll break any day now. You'll see. Then the oats'll freshen up and the sheep'll look better."

"But it's been going on like this for more than a year," said Mr Henschke. "I can't remember anything like it."

"What about 1902?" said Dad.

"Yes, that was a bad year," said Mr Craik. "But this is worse. If it doesn't break soon, I'll have to sell up."

"Don't do that, Bert," said Mr Morison, clapping him on the shoulder. "Hang on! Just hang on! The rain's coming. I can feel it in me bones."

All the men laughed. They knew about Mr Morison's bones. He was always predicting weather from the feeling in his bones but he was generally wrong. Most of them looked worried although they were laughing.

Mr Henschke had finished his mug of tea. He wandered off around the playground and collected up all the empty billies and their lids. He took each one back to the right mother. I wondered how he knew which blackened billy belonged to which family — they all looked much the same to me — but I suppose he'd seen them all so often over the years.

I went to sit with Ruth by the fence. The mothers drove off home taking the youngest children with them. Everything was ready now for the great moment — the big pull. The fathers mounted their horses and waited well out on the Track. The bullockies whirled their whips and let the thongs crack.

"Heave away, there!" shouted Mac. "Pull, you devils! Pull!"

The thirty bullocks bent their heavy shoulders to the yokes and began to pull. The men all yelled their encouragement. We screamed with excitement. Mr Mallorie even let go of his trouser-legs for a minute to wave the teams forward.

The little white school began to roll. Inch by inch it moved over the playground and out onto Gillespie's Track. Slowly the bullocks turned their heads towards Deepwater. The building edged along the rutted roadway, tilting a little from time to time so that I gasped in alarm but never quite sliding off its wheels. Ruth and I followed behind on Star. Fred Henschke had climbed up with his brother Hans. Some of the others were riding in twos and threes on horseback and the rest were running. None of us had ever seen anything so strange as this — a school sailing over the land like a ship at sea.

I looked back at the old foundations where they stood in the middle of the empty playground, at the pile of desks and pictures under the trees and at the heap of red bricks where the fireplace had once been. I felt sad. The whole place seemed desolate. But if you pass that paddock today it's rich grazing land again with not a sign that there'd ever been a school standing there, apart from the row of leaning pines along the back fence.

At the new site at Deepwater, the freshly-built timber foundations were ready and waiting in their paddock. The bullocks had to be cajoled into shuffling backwards and forwards to try to push the school into place. The drivers shouted and swore at the beasts and at each other. I began to think they'd never manage to move the building exactly where they wanted it. They tried again and again. Just as the sun was dropping down behind the western ridge, they got it right at last. The thirty bullocks were loosened from the long poles and Mac led them away to the shrunken river for a drink. The farmers set up the jacks under the building again and pulled out the bogies. Gently the school was lowered onto its blocks. There it sat, facing outwards to Gillespie's Track again with its back to the river. Not one window had been broken.

"Hurray!" shouted the weary crowd.

"Let's call it a day," said Dad. "We'll finish it off tomorrow."

The next day when we hurried down to the dry paddock by the river, Mac and his bullocks had gone. The school looked strange and unfamiliar in its new playground. The men crawled underneath again and hammered the building firmly into place. No wind or flood could move it now. The flag-pole was set up in front and a new fence built with astonishing speed by all the men working together. Dad and Mr Henschke and a couple of farmers from Kanyul dug the holes; the Douglases and the Morisons bored the wood and everyone else strained the wire from post to post and twisted it into place. That was a job every farmer in our valley knew how to do. The old white gate was hung across the entrance and the bigger boys brought along the bricks for the fireplace and chimney in a heavy cart. The shelter-shed and the two little lavatories arrived on the next cart and the desks and pictures came last of all. Ruth carried the globe into the school-room and I put the tray of inkwells carefully back on the teacher's desk. Everything was ready for the new term to start a week later when Mr Edwards would be back from his holiday down south.

When we came into the house at the end of that second day of the move, a telegram was waiting for Dad. Mother had collected it at the post office in the store when she'd gone in to buy some flour and to ask for any letters. She hadn't liked to open it till Dad was in so she'd propped it up by the clock on the mantelpiece in the kitchen. My eye caught it the minute we walked in the back door. Dad saw it too.

"A telegram!" he said, his voice suddenly harsh with anxiety.

"Is it Laurie?" I asked, putting into words what Mother was fearing.

"There's no black edge to the envelope," she said hopefully, "and anyway, I'm sure he's still in Melbourne. Nothing could've happened to him yet."

Dad tore open the telegram, his big hands shaking.

"It's not Laurie!" he said and laughed out loud with relief.

"What is it then?" asked Mother. She'd been standing close up to the fire-stove, her hands gripping her brown apron. Now her fingers relaxed.

"It's the teacher! The Schoolie! Ron Edwards! He's not coming back next week! He's joined up!"

"Not coming back?" I said. "But who'll teach all those little kids?"

"There's a new one coming," said Dad and he read out the end of the telegram from the Education Department. "R. S. Playfair arriving Wallaceville Friday afternoon train. Please meet."

"Playfair!" I laughed. "Not a bad name for a teacher! Will he live with us?"

"I suppose so," said Dad. "We can pack up Ron's things in a couple of boxes till he sends for them. I expect they could go down to his mother in St Kilda. He won't be wanting to cart all those books off to France, will he?"

The Schoolies always boarded with us. We had a spare room off the back verandah. There'd been three I could remember — Mr Edwards and two others before him. I was sorry Mr Edwards wasn't coming back. I liked him. He and Laurie always got on well too. He was a good teacher and when the weekends came round he let me borrow some of his books. I'd been thinking all day how pleased he was going to be when he saw his school at Deepwater. He wouldn't have to walk nearly so far every morning. But now he wasn't coming back at all.

"I could look after his books, Mother," I offered. "Just till the war's over. He'd never mind. He always said I could read them."

Mother looked uncertain.

"Maybe," said Dad. "We'll write off and ask him. But don't you touch them till we hear, Char. They can go into the barn in the meantime. It's as dry as a bone in there."

"And who's this R. S. Playfair, Dad?" I asked.

"Goodness only knows. I haven't any idea till I see him at the station. You can come with me on Friday, Char."

"He might bring more books," I said.

"But he mightn't want you to read them," said Mother. "Just wait till he says you can. He's bound to be different from Mr Edwards. That Mr Edwards was a nice man. A pleasure to have in the house. He always took his sheets off the bed on changing day and folded them up for me. That's what I call a gentleman. We can't be sure about this new one."

"You always fear the worst, Em," said Dad, smiling at her.

Mother smiled back.

"And I'm generally right," she said. "Remember what I said about the rain? There's hardly been a drop for months."

"Well, I'm sure this Playfair fellow'll be likeable enough. They wouldn't send a complete no-hoper up here to the Kanyul school, would they?"

"The Deepwater school, Dad!" I said. "They'll have to change its name now. It's four miles from Kanyul."

"Why isn't he in the army?" asked Mother suspiciously. She obviously wasn't too happy about R. S. Playfair.

"Health, probably," said Dad. "Short-sighted, maybe."

"Or a limp!" I suggested gloomily.

"We'll just have to wait till Friday to find out," said Dad, getting up and stretching himself. "Then we'll know it all."

2. The New Schoolie

Later that week I helped Mother pack away all Mr Edwards's things into four orange-boxes and Dad carried them into the barn. Mother gave the Schoolie's room a good clean out. I hung the floor rug over the line in the back yard and beat it with the broom handle to send the dust flying. We made up the bed with fresh sheets and put out a clean white towel. I even picked a few sprigs of wattle and stuck them in a jam-jar of water for R. S. Playfair. I wanted him to like me so I could read his books. The wattle smelt powdery and sweet.

"I do hope the poor boy will feel at home here," said Mother, gazing round the room when we'd finished. "He'll be sure to miss his mother. He's probably quite young."

"Or very old," I said. "Too old to fight. The young ones are all going off to the war."

Mother looked worried at the idea of someone very old coming to stay in the Schoolie's room.

"Char!" called Dad from the separating shed. "I need you out here. You've been fussing over that room too long. Come on!"

I left Mother to her worries and went to start skimming off the cream from the flat round pans of rich milk in the cool shed. That was a job I liked. But each week our cows were giving us less milk. I found myself hoping that Mr Morison's bones were right for once and that a great downpour was on its way.

On Friday afternoon I took off my dirty farm boots outside the door and had a good wash. Mother was very proud of her wash-house out in the back yard where we washed ourselves as well as the clothes. She had a copper in there for boiling up the sheets and shirts, two troughs and a wringer. In one corner was a cold shower. We filled the bucket with water, hoisted it up to the ceiling with a rope, pulled a chain and the chilly water cascaded down. Or that's what we did in the good years. In times of drought, when the tank was empty, showers were out of the question. We just had to make do with a wash all over every day with a small basin of creek water. I hoped the teacher wasn't going to object to that. He'd be used to two showers a day in the city. Dad would have to tell him.

I changed into clean clothes for the drive into Wallaceville. My hair was always pulled tight into plaits for the farm work but that day I brushed it all out so it hung almost to my waist — mouse-coloured and crinkled. I looked like a proper farmer's daughter now and not like Dad's right-hand woman. I wanted to make a good impression on Mr Playfair. Dad was quite spruced up himself. He looked as if he was off to church. Mother smiled at us in approval.

'Wallaceville' was too much of a mouthful for everyday use. Most of us just called it 'Wally'. I hadn't been there very often but I had high hopes that Dad was going to let me join him on the days when he went into town with Mr Henschke or Mr Morison to sell his lambs or buy some new calves for fattening. My hopes came to nothing. He said he didn't want me anywhere near those pubs where the farmers gathered for a drink after the cattle sales. But he was quite happy to let me come to meet the new Schoolie.

"You do need to see a bit of the world, Char!" he said as we climbed into the buggy. Dad's horse Fly was between the shafts for the long bumpy ride to town. The dust flew up from Gillespie's Track. Generally there'd still be muddy patches in September but not that year. We had to skirt around the dry pot holes by driving right up onto the rough verges.

The Track followed the course of the river the whole way into town. One well-kept farm led on to the next on our western side of the river. There was hardly a break between them. First there was the little knot of farms at our top end — Deepwater — with the newly-shifted school and the general store. Then four miles down the Track came Kanyul with another store and a little church. Presbyterian, of course. Our whole valley was Presbyterian, pretty well. That Kanyul church was where we went on Sundays — walking or riding on the good days and taking the buggy if the heat was quite unbearable. I knew all those little farms within a few miles of the church but beyond that I was in less familiar country. Burnett's Bridge was the next settlement and then Longstone Bend and Talisker before we came to Wally.

Every farm in our valley was very much like the next. We all went in for mixed farming. In a good year there'd be the lush grasslands for the dairy cattle and the calves along the river but that year the grass was looking brown as early as July. Big clumps of stringybark and peppermint stood in the paddocks for shade. Beyond the flat grass, on the lower slopes of the hill, we grew our crops. Oats mainly but some wheat as well. The homesteads were here too and the milking sheds and the barns. Towards the top of the ridge lay the rougher sheep country — tough wiry grass and bracken and patches of wild scrub. It was a stiff climb up there after the sheep but I did it often enough in those war years. At lambing time we'd bring the ewes down the hill so we could keep a good eye on them. From the very top of that ridge you could look right along the valley with its silver dams shining in the sunlight and its long winding river. You could see the roofs of the farm-houses and the out-buildings and the orchards of apple and walnut.

That was our side of the valley. The quiet side. The tamed side. But across the river to the east you could see the wild side. That was another world over there. There wasn't any Gillespie's Track on the far side and no other kind of track either. The hills over there were much too steep for farming, even for sheep, and the thick bush had been left quite untouched. Ruth Henschke and I used to think that everything over there looked far more exciting than on our side. That would be the place to go exploring or looking for gold or hiding out for months at a time. It was mountain-ash country with all the giant trees still standing. Dad used to say there'd be lyre-birds in among the damp tree-ferns in the gullies. There'd be even more kangaroos and wallabies and wombats than we saw round the farm. Only the birds ever crossed the river from the forest to the farmland — the cockatoos and the king parrots, the currawongs and the thornbills, the ibis and the blue cranes.

At the railway station in Wally a little crowd was gathering already to meet the afternoon train. Not that there was any morning train. The afternoon train came up from the city just three days a week — Mondays, Wednesdays and Fridays. Dad nodded to a few men he knew. We could hear the pulse of the engine as it came up the line towards us from the mysterious south. When it thundered into the station, its pistons slowing and its steam hissing, I pressed well back against the picket fence. All the doors swung open in one movement and the passengers jumped down. I rushed forward to Dad's side and scanned their faces, trying to work out which one was the new Schoolie. I wanted to be sure to spot him before Dad did. I wanted to be able to shout out, "Look, Dad! There he is! That must be him!"

But I couldn't see him at all.

Most of the passengers had been claimed by eager relatives. There was no one short-sighted and no one with a limp. No one very old either. In fact the only person left standing there with a suitcase was a young woman — a girl I almost said. She only looked about twenty though she might have been more. Her eyes searched the crowd anxiously. She saw Dad turning his head this way and that and she approached him hesitantly.

"Excuse me," she said. "You're not Mr Ross from Deepwater by any chance, are you?"

"I am," he said, staring at her.

"I'm the new teacher. I'm Miss Playfair."

"*Miss* Playfair!" exclaimed Dad. He was astonished. "But it's always been a man!"

"I know. I'm sorry. I do hope you won't mind. The men are all off to the war, you see. So I was told to come."

Dad recovered quickly but his surprise still showed. He seemed embarrassed. He talked far too fast.

"No, no, of course not. Don't mind a bit. The wife'll be glad

21

of the company, I'm sure. This is Charlotte. The boy's in the army. Come on, now. Give me your case, Miss. The buggy's just outside."

Miss Playfair! I was too stunned to speak. I contented myself with looking closely at her long tweed skirt and her brown velvet jacket. Such splendid clothes had never been seen in our valley, not even on Sundays when we all wore our best to church. I couldn't quite catch a glimpse of the colour of her hair — it was all stuffed up inside a remarkable blue felt hat with a little feather in the band at one side. Her skin seemed unusually pale to me but perhaps city people all looked like that. She moved gracefully. She almost floated over the ground.

What on earth would the kids at the school make of this fragile goddess of a teacher? How ever would she keep the boys in order? I couldn't see her wielding Mr Edwards's strap with much force. There'd be bedlam in that school room at Deepwater from now on!

And how could she possibly eat her breakfast and her tea in our kitchen with the old red oil-cloth on the table and the black stove beside her? The kitchen was the heart of our house. We ate there and we sat there to talk. We lived there. There was a tiny front room with Mother's best lace cloth on a round table and a hard leather sofa but we almost never went in there. We called it the front room or sometimes the parlour. That was kept for best and in my experience best never seemed to happen. The other farmhouses in the valley were all the same though the Henschkes did use their parlour at Christmas. This Miss Playfair didn't look as if she was used to meals in the kitchen. She was city, through and through.

Miss Playfair was silent for most of the journey home and so was Dad. They didn't seem to know what to say. So I started talking and once I'd started I couldn't stop. I pointed out all the farms as we passed them and I told her the name of each little settlement. I talked about Mr Edwards and how we liked him and how he let me read his books. I wanted to get that bit in early. Miss Playfair kept gazing around her all the time with an excitement that she seemed to be trying to hide.

"Did you know they'd moved the school?" I asked.

She looked startled and shook her head.

"Just this week," I rushed on. "It's not at Kanyul any more. Not enough kids there. They've moved it up to Deepwater. You won't have to walk so far."

I couldn't tell what she thought of this. Her pale face didn't give much away.

"Grown up on a farm yourself, Miss Playfair?" asked Dad, breaking his long silence at last. Perhaps he wanted to stop me burbling. He glanced sideways at her as he spoke.

"No," she said. "I was born in the city. But my father grew up on a farm. Near Ballarat, it was."

Dad gave a bit of a grunt. I don't think he regarded farms near Ballarat as real farms at all.

"So your grandfather was a farmer," he said.

"No. Not exactly. He worked on a farm. He didn't own it."

Dad gave another grunt even less enthusiastic than the last.

"And what line of business is your father in now?" he persisted.

I did wish he'd stop asking all these questions. It seemed very rude to me. But Miss Playfair didn't seem to mind at all.

"He's in the railways," she said proudly. "Quite a good job. He's a clerk in the head office. He's not driving the trains or anything like that."

I coughed loudly to drown any grunts Dad might make at this piece of information. I thought driving trains would be a lot better than sitting in an office and I'm sure Dad thought so too but luckily he was silent. Miss Playfair went on.

"He's very clever, you know. My father. He wanted to be a teacher himself but it just wasn't possible. So the minute I was born he had the idea that *I'd* be a teacher. And now I am. He's very pleased. Though he's not so pleased that I've been sent up to the country."

She stopped suddenly as she realized that this wasn't the politest thing to say to Dad. Her pale skin went red.

"Is this your first job, then?" asked Dad.

"Not quite. I've had two terms in a big city school. Richmond."

"Country schools are different," said Dad.

"Yes, I know."

"I'm sure you'll like it," I said quickly. I was afraid Dad was going to put her off the Deepwater school with all these terse remarks of his. Now that this extraordinary person had come to the valley, I didn't want her to pack up and go away again.

Mother was waiting on the verandah, looking out for us along the Track. The sun was going down already. Evening came on early in the valley and morning came late. The high ridge on each side of the river blocked off the sun as it rose and set. The shadows were long. It was almost milking time. I could hear our cows mooing impatiently by the shed as we came nearer home.

Mother caught sight of the new teacher sitting up rather stiffly in the buggy between Dad and me. She gazed at all three of us in utter amazement. Her face was a mixture of pleasure and alarm. I had a fair idea what she'd be thinking. Would the Schoolie's room be too small? Would our meals be good enough? Would a woman lodger be much more trouble in the house than a man? Would the Schoolie always want to be washing herself and wasting too much of our water? At the same time she was probably thinking how much she'd enjoy this new company. Mother was friendly with all the women at our end of the valley but she didn't get out to see them much. Another woman living in the house — even such a young one — could make all the difference.

Mother ran to the front gate to meet us. She didn't often run but I remember how she ran that day.

"Whoa!" said Dad.

He pulled on the reins and the horse stopped. Mother reached up to shake hands with the new Schoolie.

"So it's *Miss* Playfair!" she said.

"Yes. Roberta Playfair. Hullo, Mrs Ross. I'm so glad to be here."

Miss Playfair climbed down, holding her skirt carefully up out of the red dust near our front gate. I was thinking about her strange name. Roberta. I'd heard of Alberta before. In fact I even had an auntie called Alberta. But I'd never heard of Roberta.

"You're very welcome," said Mother. "I do hope it won't be too rough for you out here. The room's very small, I'm afraid. We've always had a man, you see. Char'll bring your case for you. It can't be too heavy."

It was heavy. Books, I thought to myself. Books or boots. I staggered in behind Mother and Miss Playfair while Dad drove the buggy round to the stable.

"Milking time, Char!" he called to me over his shoulder.

"And here's your room," Mother was saying, looking anxiously into the teacher's face as she flung open the door off the back verandah.

Miss Playfair smiled as she looked round the room.

"It's very nice," she said.

"You'd better change, Char, and get out to the shed," said Mother.

Reluctantly I put down the case by the bed and went off to help Dad. I wished I could stay there with Mother. I knew I'd be missing all their conversation. By the time I got back from the milking, everything interesting would have been said. It was maddening.

I think I was right. No one said much over the table at tea time. Miss Playfair ate very slowly and we all had to hold back so as not to race ahead of her. I could see her hair now. In fact I kept staring at it and wondering how she kept that knot in place at the top of her head. Her hair was dark, almost black. Mother seemed fascinated by the white tucked blouse the Schoolie was wearing and by the gold locket around her neck. Dad had apparently forgotten she was there at all. His eyes were fixed on his plate. It was left to Miss Playfair herself to jolly us along with her questions about the farm, the sheep, the cows and the crops. I was the one who had to tell her it had been a bad year with almost no rain. She looked surprised. It was obviously the first she'd ever heard of the drought. Perhaps they didn't notice those things down in the city.

"And Charlotte," she said quickly, as if she didn't want to

hear any more about the dry weather. "I suppose you must be one of my older pupils."

"No," I said bluntly. "I've just left. I'm fourteen. I help Dad on the farm. Laurie's gone off to the war, you see."

Mother fidgetted in embarrassment but Miss Playfair made no comment.

A sharp knock came on the kitchen door. Mr Mallorie walked straight in without waiting for an answer. That was normal in the valley. Some people didn't even knock but just called out 'Yoo-hoo!' or 'Coo-ee' from the back verandah and then walked in. No one ever came to the front. It was always the back.

"Thought I'd drop in," said Mr Mallorie, standing there inside the door and hitching at his trouser-legs.

"Do sit down, Mr Mallorie," said Mother. I think she probably wished he'd picked another day to drop in but he was quite unpredictable. "There's still plenty of lamb stew in the pot."

She took down a white plate from the dresser and Mr Mallorie pulled up a chair to the table.

"Hullo there, Keith," said Dad. "This is the new teacher. Miss Playfair. Our neighbour, Mr Mallorie."

"Pleased to meet you," said Mr Mallorie. "I thought a man was coming."

I rushed in before Miss Playfair had to make the same old answer.

"The men are all off to the war," I said.

Mr Mallorie nodded and began to eat his stew. It was thick with meat and carrots and onions and potatoes. Now and then he looked across at Miss Playfair, examining her face carefully every time.

"Playfair?" he said at last, pausing between mouthfuls. "Unusual name that, Miss."

"It's Scottish," she said. "Or English. I'm not quite sure which."

Dad laughed.

"You don't want to mix them up," he said. "Not in this valley, anyway. There's a world of difference between Scottish and English."

"I knew a Playfair once," Mr Mallorie went on. "He was a Scot all right. Old mate of me father's. In the early days."

I felt like kicking Mr Mallorie but of course I didn't. He was always thinking he knew people. If you even said a name like 'Smith', he'd start to tell you that he'd known a Smith in the early days. And he'd be certain it was the very one you'd mentioned — or some close relation at least. Funnily enough, it often was!

"I remember him clearly," he went on. "I was just a boy then. Dad'd known him for years. Came out in the same ship."

"I don't think. . ." said Miss Playfair uncertainly, looking across at Mr Mallorie. She seemed to be trying to calculate his age.

"No," said Mr Mallorie, talking half to himself. "Couldn't be your father. Too young. Might've been your grandfather."

"I'm afraid I never knew my grandfather. He died long before I was born. There could've been other Playfairs in those early days, Mr Mallorie."

"He had a fine name and a fine head of black hair," Mr Mallorie went on as if she hadn't spoken. "Robert Somerville Playfair."

Miss Playfair's knife and fork clinked down loudly onto her plate.

"But that's almost my name!" she said, astonished. "I'm Roberta Somerville Playfair. And my father is Robert Somerville Playfair."

Mr Mallorie looked quite unsurprised.

"Must've been your grandfather. Thought as much. Same hair."

"These old Scottish families do like to keep the name going," said Mother. "Alec here is the fifth Alec Ross in his family. We made a bit of a change with Laurie. It was too confusing."

"Where exactly was it you knew my grandfather, Mr Mallorie?" Miss Playfair asked. "Was it near Ballarat? That's where he lived when my father was born."

"No. Not Ballarat. Eaglehawk. People moved around a lot

in them days, you know." Mr Mallorie paused and then he added. "He give me a stone once."

"A stone!" I laughed. "That's a funny present! There's stones everywhere!"

"Not like this one, lass. This stone's different. I've still got it up there at the hut. There's a hole right through the middle and a little pebble wedged in the hole. Nothink'll get it out. I used to try when I was a lad in Eaglehawk. Even took a hammer to it once till me mother stopped me. Yes, he was a great one for the stones, Bob Playfair. Collected 'em."

Miss Playfair still hadn't quite got used to the idea that this odd old Mr Mallorie really had known her grandfather but she tried to go on making polite conversation to cover up her surprise.

"I'll write and tell my father I've met you, Mr Mallorie," she said brightly. "He'll be so pleased. He's always been very proud of his father. He often talks about him though I think he died when my father was only a boy." She turned to Mother. "My grandfather was going to be a minister, you see, Mrs Ross. In the church. Back in Scotland or wherever it was. But then he developed some throat trouble. 'A weakness of the throat' my father always calls it. The doctor said he should go to the colonies. For the warmer climate. So he had to give up his studies straight away and take a berth in one of the sailing ships."

"How sad," said Mother.

"But he got such a good job on the ship, Mrs Ross. He was the tutor to two little boys. He taught them Latin, my father says."

"There was nothink wrong with his throat when I knew him," said Mr Mallorie. "The sun must've fixed it. Yes, a great man for the stones."

"I do hope you like rice pudding, Miss Playfair," said Mother, changing the subject. "Mr Edwards was always very fond of it."

"Oh yes, I do, thank you," said Miss Playfair.

"Made with our own milk and cream," said Mother proudly as she put the browned pudding on the table.

"And full of raisins," I added.

"I was hoping it'd be rice pudding, Mrs Ross," said Mr Mallorie. "I always like to pick rice pudding days if I can."

"There's enough for second helpings, so eat up, everyone," said Mother.

Mr Mallorie, as usual, took Mother at her word. His dish was empty before Miss Playfair had half-finished hers. She was a slow eater all right. Chewed every mouthful thirty-two times, the way you're supposed to, though we never bothered. There's not much point in chewing rice pudding thirty-two times. I was beginning to think she might be a bit finicky. But perhaps she was just distracted by Mr Mallorie. She certainly kept gazing across at him as if she couldn't quite believe her eyes. I was so used to him that I'd hardly ever bothered to look at him properly. I looked now. I tried to see him as she must be seeing him. He was a strange-looking man, even when he wasn't shuffling along the Track and hitching up his trouser-legs. Dad had often told me that he wasn't as old as he seemed. Well, he looked about eighty to me! Not that I had much idea of age then. I used to think Dad was terribly old though he was probably only forty. So perhaps Mr Mallorie was more like sixty — or seventy perhaps. Who knows? His shoulders were hunched and his hair was completely white. Thin and white. His hands were blotched brown from years of sun and the blue veins stood out in criss-cross patterns across their backs. That wasn't unusual. Most of our farmers had hands like that. My eyes went back to his face. His teeth! That was it! He had hardly any teeth at all! Two in the front at the top and perhaps a couple at the back. The rest was gaping gum. No wonder he was so fond of rice pudding. He could just swallow without chewing. The wonder was that he talked as plainly as he did with so few teeth to help him.

Miss Playfair went to bed early that first night. She was tired. I helped Mother with the dishes. Then I carried out the tin dish full of dirty water to pour over the vegetables in the dark garden. We had to use every scrap and never waste a drop. Dad yarned away with Mr Mallorie.

3. The War Comes Closer

The next morning Dad said I could take some time off to show Miss Playfair the school. We kept the key at our place. There wasn't any caretaker, of course. The mothers took it in turns to sweep the room out once a week. That's all the cleaning it ever got.

Miss Playfair had on a different skirt that day. Greyish. And a different white blouse too but the same locket round her neck. I wondered what was inside. A strand of her mother's hair, perhaps? She'd never mentioned her mother. Or a portrait of some young man in soldier's uniform? Or of the father she talked about so much? Or even of the grandfather? I couldn't very well ask her. I wished I had a locket myself. In fact, as I walked down to the school beside Miss Playfair that Saturday morning, I found there were a lot of things that I wished I had. A soft grey skirt, for one thing, and black hair with a knot on top, and pale skin and a walk that was a kind of glide. I felt very awkward with my mouse-coloured hair in tight plaits and my grubby cotton skirt hanging a few inches below my knees and my boots that clumped along in the dust.

I unlocked the door and let Miss Playfair in. Luckily, she didn't really seem to notice me or my clothes much. She was far more interested in the room. She dashed about excitedly, twirling the globe on its stand and looking up at the pictures on the wall. She sat in the big chair at the teacher's desk and then she stood up again and sat down again. She found a broken bit of chalk in the drawer and wrote Monday's date carefully on the blackboard.

"Where are all the slates, Charlotte?" she asked me.

30

"The kids bring their own," I said. "You'll see them on Monday. Everyone has two little bits of cloth. One wet and one dry. For cleaning the slates. You can always get new slate-pencils at Pollock's store."

I must admit I didn't much miss the squeak of slate-pencils or the smell of those damp cleaning cloths. That was something I'd put behind me forever now. Miss Playfair was welcome to it. But in other ways I wished I was going to be there with Ruth and the others on Monday morning.

I left Miss Playfair to arrange the room the way she wanted it and to pin up some new maps she'd brought with her. I went to find Dad. We were planting out vegetables that morning — tomatoes and beans and lettuce — and carrying water to them from the creek. There were lambs to be sorted out for the next week's sale, too. I hated to see them go but Dad was relentless. Farming was a hard-headed business, he told me. It took me years to learn.

I ran down to the Henschkes' farm after tea to tell Ruth about the new Schoolie. She'd heard already. I suppose the whole valley knew by that time. But she hadn't heard about the lovely blouses or the locket and she didn't know anything about the clever father in the railways or the grandfather with the throat. I had lots to tell her. She didn't say much. She was sad about Mr Edwards. She really liked him. We all did.

Miss Playfair came to church with us on the Sunday. She said she was really Church of England but when she heard that the nearest one was twenty miles off she realized she'd just have to make do with the Presbyterian. Dad drove the buggy though the day wasn't very hot. I think he wondered if Miss Playfair could manage to walk four miles. We were the centre of everyone's attention at the church as we sat in our usual pew with the new Schoolie between Mother and me. I could hear the whispers going round in the seats behind us as people worked out who she was and the kids started giggling about what they'd get up to on Monday. I turned my head to look at Ruth. She nodded and smiled and then her eyes went back to Miss Playfair. The minister didn't get much of a hearing that Sunday. He'd ridden all the way out from Wally, brisk and cheerful as usual. He'd take another service at Burnett's Bridge late in the afternoon and then ride back to town. It wasn't our turn to have him to lunch — he was off to the Henschkes that Sunday. He seemed as curious as everyone else about the new teacher. I even saw him open his eyes in the middle of one of his prayers just to have a good look at her!

I walked back from church on my own and let the others go ahead in the buggy. I wanted to practise that gliding stride. By the time I'd reached the farm gate I'd mastered it but the minute I walked in at the kitchen door I found I'd gone back to my usual half-run.

"Come on, Char!" said Mother. "We've had to start without you. I've never known you take so long. You'd better ride next week."

"Can you ride, Miss Playfair?" I asked as I sat down.

She shook her head.

"I could teach you," I offered. "Star's very gentle."

Miss Playfair didn't look enthusiastic but she thanked me politely.

"Just wait a few weeks," said Mother to me. "Miss Playfair has to get used to her school first and all those little children. The riding can come later."

The new teacher smiled across at her, greatly relieved.

"Charlotte could tell me about the children," she said.

So I could, I thought, thinking of Fred Henschke and Ken Douglas and Jack Morison! But it might be better if I didn't tell her too much. She might get scared.

In fact, Miss Playfair's first day in the school passed off without any kind of trouble. The kids were all excited by this lovely new teacher and they sat as quiet as mice, folding their hands up on their heads whenever she told them to and offering to fill the ink-wells and put the flowers in water and to clean the blackboard. Even Fred was a model of helpfulness. She came home delighted with it all and she talked on and on about the school and the children as we ate our tea.

"But they don't seem to know much about the war, Mr Ross," she said to Dad.

"No. I don't suppose they would. It hasn't been going long

and it's all so far off. Most of them probably don't even know there is a war yet."

"I'll have to change all that," she said. "I've brought a map of Europe up from the city with me and lots of little flags. We can move the British flags each day so the children will see how we're winning."

"What if we don't win?" I asked.

"Oh, we're sure to win, Charlotte," she said firmly. "We've got right on our side, you see. Right must triumph. And it won't be long. My father says it'll be all over by Christmas."

"I do hope so," said Mother, thinking of Laurie.

"We don't get the war news very quickly up here," said Dad. "The farming paper only comes once a week and it's full of the drought. We often don't know what's going on over there."

"I'll just have ask my father to write to tell me the war news," she said. "He reads two papers every day."

Dad had no reply to this extraordinary bit of information. Two papers a day! When did the man get his work done?

"I thought I'd teach the children some patriotic songs," Miss Playfair went on. "And I want them to start raising some money for the Comforts Fund for the poor soldiers. And knitting, of course. I suppose all the girls can knit, can they, Charlotte?"

"Most of them can. The Henschke girls are the best. They knit a funny way that their mother taught them. They hold the needles differently. But they go much faster than anyone else."

"Well, I'll have to teach them all to knit the proper way and then we can make scarves for the soldiers."

"How can you raise money for the Comforts Fund, Miss Playfair?" I asked.

"That's quite easy. All the schools down south are doing it now. The children can grow vegetables or flowers and sell them. Or keep hens and sell the eggs. Or offer to do jobs for the neighbours."

"But everyone here grows vegetables and keeps chooks anyway," said Mother, looking worried. "I don't think

33

anyone'd be willing to pay for them."

"I'm sure they will when they know it's all for a good cause," said Miss Playfair. "And the great thing is it will help the children to take a real interest in the war. It brings the war closer, you see. I could send a letter to the parents to explain it all, Mrs Ross."

"Good idea," said Dad, but I didn't think he looked very enthusiastic.

That evening I helped Miss Playfair make more of her little flags for the map. It was the first of many happy evenings I spent that way. I loved helping her. The flags weren't hard to make. I got quite good at doing tiny union-jacks with the strips of red, white and blue in just the right places. Miss Playfair gave me a big one to copy from. The German flags were easy. They were just black. Every flag was fixed to a pin so it could be stuck into the map at school. She'd brought a whole box of pins with her.

Miss Playfair's plan did seem to work well. The kids enjoyed moving the flags and singing the songs. Within a couple of weeks, thick skeins of khaki-coloured wool had arrived in an enormous parcel from the city and all the girls began on the scarves. I even offered to do one myself. I wanted to please her and she certainly was pleased. I could only knit in the evenings after the day's work on the farm and I was often too tired to do more than a few rows. I used to fall into bed at eight o'clock most nights in those first few months of farm work so my scarf progressed very slowly. I was afraid the war would be well over before I'd finished it.

Miss Playfair even had a great success with her idea of raising money for the Comforts Funds. She wrote out her letter to the parents eight times — that was the number of families if you count the ones at Kanyul as well as the ones at Deepwater — and the children carried them home. Soon every child had a chook or a strip of garden or a beehive. All the fathers were generous in handing over something on the farm so every kid could raise a bit of money for the soldiers. Generally it was the mothers who had to pay for the eggs or the honey or the vegetables but no one minded. The kids were really keen, carrying heavy buckets of water all the way from the river to pour over their precious vegetable strips. The Pollocks at the store didn't have much of a garden so Sid and Annie offered to do deliveries at a penny a time. That went well too. And we needn't have worried about how Miss Playfair would manage the kids in the school. They all liked her so much and they were so enthusiastic about winning the war that she didn't ever need to get out Mr Edwards's strap from the drawer in her desk where it lay curled up like a sleeping snake. She was right. She brought the war nearer.

At the end of September we had a happy letter from Laurie. He still hadn't sailed yet but he was enjoying the army life. He said he was learning how to use his gun and his bayonet and how to march up and down in straight lines and to look all neat and tidy for the war. He said it was lucky he could ride. That was going to be useful. He'd made lots of new friends from other parts of the State, mostly country boys, and he told us all about the fun they had in the barracks, singing songs in the evening and playing tricks on each other.

"Boys will be boys," said Mother proudly when she'd read the letter aloud to us for the third time on the day it came. Miss Playfair asked if she could take it to school to read to the children and Mother said yes. I think it had its effect too. The children must've reported the letter at home and a week later Gordon Craik went off to the city to enlist. Mr Craik was going to find it hard to run his big farm with only Bill left at home (apart from the five little ones) but he was just as proud as Dad that his boy was helping to win the war.

In early October, Mother and I went with Dad to the Show at Wally. It was a pathetic affair that year. Some of the farmers had been hit so hard by the lack of rain that they didn't enter any of their animals at all. We had some ewes to show but they were pretty scraggy compared with the ones we usually had. We won a third prize but there wasn't much pleasure walking round the half-empty pens to look at the other farmers' heifers and bulls and sheep. Even the butter entries were disappointing. Too pale. The vegetables were drooping and weary. Only the tent for the cake competitions held much interest. The cooks had not been put off by the drought. Mrs Henschke had won a first prize for her fruit cake and another for her sponge. Mother was as pleased as if she'd won them herself.

We sold off most of our calves that month but we didn't get much of a price for them. I missed them when they'd gone — their soft muzzles and their big eyes and their friendly licking tongues. But Dad said we'd soon be starting on the hay-making and then I'd forget the calves in sheer exhaustion. He was right. I did.

Miss Playfair had settled easily into our house. She wasn't any trouble. She was careful with the water and always tipped it on the garden after her morning wash, just the way we did. Mother really liked her. And I was still fascinated. More than fascinated. Almost obsessed. I tried to copy not just the way she walked but her voice too and the words she liked to use. I started to say 'my father says' instead of 'Dad reckons' and I talked of 'the children' instead of 'the kids' — when I remembered. In my bedroom at night, when the door was shut, I practised putting up my hair into a twisted knot like the one on Miss Playfair's head. I couldn't do it properly but I kept on trying — brushing, combing, coiling and pinning — again and again. I even started to learn some of the poems she was teaching the children now that they'd learnt all the songs. Poems about England and how much we loved her. I'd never thought much about England. Scotland was the only country I knew about, apart from Australia, and I really didn't know much about Scotland. But now I had a passion for England. I would have died for her, I told myself. I was longing for the day when I'd be old enough to go to the war myself as a Red Cross nurse. I was going to be the Australian Florence Nightingale and I could see myself gliding from bed to bed, murmuring words of comfort to the dying soldiers.

No rain fell in October. Not one drop. Our creek was reduced to a string of muddy holes. I found the first dead sheep that month. She lay stiff and cold near the top of the ridge. There was no more grass to eat. She was to be the first of many. Dad had to dig a trench to bury them. We lost two of our best milkers a few weeks later. You could count every one of their ribs. We had to burn the carcases. The other farmers were digging their trenches too and burning their dead cattle. The wind kept blowing on and off from the north — hot and dry across the paddocks. And that was the month when the first sign of trouble at the school began to start.

One Wednesday morning Mrs Henschke came up to see Mother. I watched her walking slowly in the heat, waving away the flies with both her hands. She and Mother sat talking for hours in the kitchen. She stayed on into the afternoon. Every time I barged in I saw Mrs Henschke sitting there crying. And every time Mother said, "Not just now, Char," and I had to go out again.

Mother put some sandwiches outside the door for Dad and me. I told him about Mrs Henschke.

"Do you think she's having another baby, Dad?" I asked him.

"No, no," he said sharply, brushing this aside in embarrassment. "It must be the farm. Things must be bad down there. Their creek's not as good as ours. Maybe it's run dry altogether. I'd better go down and see Dan Henschke. He could be going bust, poor bloke. And he won't be the last. This whole valley's going bust, I reckon."

"Don't go just yet, Dad," I said. "Let's wait and see what Mother says. It might not be the farm at all. It could be some terrible illness Mrs Henschke's got. I think she's looking thinner."

Mother said not a word about Mrs Henschke at tea time that evening. She just chatted on to Miss Playfair about the school. Dad and I had to be patient. We had to wait till half way through the next morning when we came into the kitchen for a cup of tea and a breather.

"What was the matter with Mrs Henschke, Mother?" I asked.

Then she told us.

There were three problems really though I think they were all connected. First of all, there was Martin. He was the eldest and he was down in the city.

37

"He's gone and changed his name!" said Mother. "Changed his name to Brown!"

"Why? What's wrong with Henschke?" I asked.

"It's a German name. He went to enlist and he was told they don't want Germans in the Australian army. He's desperate to get to the war like everyone else. So he's changed his name. He's Martin Brown. And the army's accepted him now."

"How can anyone change their name?" I asked. "It's not possible."

"You do it by deed poll," said Dad. "It's not difficult. I must say I think he could've picked something a bit better than Brown! Every Tom, Dick and Harry's called Brown!"

"I suppose that's just why he wanted it," said Mother. "But Mrs Henschke is very upset and I don't blame her. She's proud of that old family name, just the way we're proud of Ross. They've been good Australians for two generations now. It's only Martin's grandparents who were really German — on both sides of the family — and all four of them are dead anyway. The Henschkes were born here. Just like us."

"It's not fair!" I blurted out.

"And that's not all. There's Ruth and Lisa and Kate," said Mother. "They're in trouble too."

I've told you that Ruth was my best friend. There's a lot more to say about her but I'll come to that soon. She was fourteen, just like me, and we'd been right up through the Kanyul school together, along with her twin brother Bernie. He'd left school back in March and gone into Wally to start his apprenticeship as a carpenter with Mr McDonald. He boarded in there and only came home about once a month. We didn't see much of him any more. Ruth was staying on at the school for the last term after I left so she was the only one of the three of us still going there. She missed me, she said, and of course she missed Bernie too. I certainly missed her. I saw her only once or twice a week now instead of every day. Lisa was thirteen and Kate was eleven.

"It's the knitting," said Mother. "You know those three Henschke girls are the best knitters in the school. Well, our

Miss Playfair has told them they've got to knit 'properly'. She laughed out loud at that strange way they hold their needles. She says it must be the German way and they have to stop. She asked them what their mother's name was before she married and when they said 'Wolf' she laughed again and said she'd thought as much. So they've tried to change the way they knit and they just can't manage it. Their fingers keep going the way they're used to. Then all the other kids in the school laugh at them and Miss Playfair makes them pull it all out and start again. They're the slowest in the school now instead of the fastest. Lisa and Kate are coming home in tears every day with their wool in a terrible tangle. Mrs Henschke sorts it out for them but they always end up with the same tangle the next day."

"What about Ruth?" I asked. "She hasn't said a thing to me."

"She doesn't cry like the others but her knitting is in just the same mess. She's refusing to go to school, Mrs Henschke says."

"It's ridiculous!" said Dad angrily. "You'll have to speak to Miss Playfair, Em. You can make her see sense!"

"Wait on, Alec," said Mother. "There's more to come. The puppets!"

Every year as long as anyone could remember, Mr Henschke had taken his puppets to the school for the Christmas party. He had four of them and they were very old. They had big wooden heads, beautifully carved and painted. They were so old the paint was cracking. I think his father had brought them out in the early days. There was Kasper and the Grandma and Gretchen and the Wicked Robber. We loved them and we'd watched them every Christmas all our lives. Mr Henschke used to carry them to the school in a big square pack on his back and then the pack folded out into a little theatre that he used to set up on the teacher's desk. Then he'd stand hidden behind it and move the puppets across the stage, two at a time. And he'd do all the voices himself too. Every voice was different and we completely forgot that it was really just Mr Henschke doing them all. I somehow believed that those puppets were real people who could really talk, even though I knew perfectly well that Mr Henschke had his hand inside each one in turn and was making the voices in behind the little theatre. The puppets acted the same old plays every year and we never got tired of watching them.

"Miss Playfair's told Ruth that the school won't be needing the puppets this Christmas," Mother went on. "She says they're not suitable. Because of the war. She's going to have a Pageant instead."

"What's that?" I asked.

"It's a kind of play. And it's going to be about the Empire. England and the Empire. And the war. She's going to dress up all the children to be different countries. And I think one of those songs comes into it too. She told Ruth that they might have the puppets another year."

"But the kids in the school'll never put up with that!" I said. "They'll want the puppets!"

"That's the odd thing, Char. They don't want the puppets. They're all siding with Miss Playfair. And some of them have even started shouting 'Hun' and 'Bosch' and 'Kraut' at the Henschkes in the playground. Wherever did they learn such words?"

"Miss Playfair'll have to stop that," said Dad fiercely, "or I'll stop it myself!"

"She's tried, Mrs Henschke says. She's told the school that the Henschkes are all good little Australians and no one must tease them. But the name-calling still goes on when she's not around."

"But she started the whole thing!" I said. "With the knitting and the puppets! She put the idea in their heads!"

"You'll have to talk to her, Alec," said Mother. "I can't do it."

"I suppose I will," he said. "But I'll go and see Dan Henschke first of all. That bloke must be worried. This new Schoolie's stirred up a hornet's nest."

And I'd thought she was so lovely. I still did. That was the trouble. I didn't quite know what I felt about her now.

"Poor Mrs Henschke!" said Mother.

"They'll all be changing their name to Brown soon!" I said gloomily.

At tea that night I didn't gaze across the table at Miss Playfair's locket. I kept my eyes on my plate. When she asked me to help her with the flags, I made an excuse. I was too tired, I said. I went off to bed at half past seven. Mother let me get one of Mr Edwards's books out of the box in the barn to read in bed. Just this once, she said.

4. Bernie

Dad did talk to Miss Playfair the next day. What exactly he said I don't know. He went to see her at the school at lunch time. That would be easier than trying to say something over the table at home with Mother and me sitting there too. Miss Playfair agreed to let him speak to all the kids in the school. He told them that there was to be no more taunting of the Henschkes. No more words like Hun and Bosch.

"But will they take any notice of you, Dad?" I asked as we were doing the milking together that night. I pressed my face against the cow's flank and pulled harder on her teats. The milk — what there was of it — hissed into the bucket in a thin stream.

"I don't know," said Dad from the next stall. "Those kids didn't look me in the eye. None of them did. They just sat there in their desks and kept glancing at each other in a shifty sort of way. The Henschkes looked as if they wanted to run out of the room. Lisa was crying. I think I've only made things worse by barging in there. I didn't like the feeling in that school room, Char. It was nasty."

"You had to do something, Dad. What about Miss Playfair?"

"She was very nice. Quite agreed with me really. But she won't give way on the knitting. She says she has her standards. The Henschkes have to knit properly."

"What did she say about the puppets?"

"I didn't mention the puppets."

"Dad! That's the most important thing!"

Dad sighed.

"I've done the best I can, Char," he said. "Off you go,

Polly!" And he slapped the cow gently on her rump and let her out of the stall. "Come on now, Sukey! Your turn next."

There was a lull for a few weeks at Deepwater. The Henschke girls began to manage their knitting better. The name-calling in the school had died down. Dad's stern words must have had more effect than he thought they would. He hadn't made things worse, anyway.

In early November a couple of shearers came to lend Dad a hand with the wool clip. They were camping on the other side of the sheds and they had all their meals in the kitchen with us. Cheerful blokes they were but, as Dad said about the shearers every year, as 'rough as bags'. Miss Playfair didn't find much to say to them nor they to her.

I was working on the hay-making. That was a job I could do on my own with Dad's heavy fork, turning the new hay over every day in the long paddock. I was slow at the job and my back ached. The grass was so dry already that the turning seemed pointless to me but Dad insisted. Although I wore a big-brimmed straw hat of Mother's to keep off the worst of the sun, my face was getting browner every day. I could see her looking at me anxiously when I came back into the house. Was I turning into an old hag already, I wondered?

When the hay was bound well and ready to stack, Dad brought his cart to the paddock and we tossed up the bundles together. The two great draught horses, Jip and Ginger, knew just when to move on and when to stop. Most years we had two lovely golden hay-stacks by the barn but we only managed one stumpy brown stack that year. It was a poor crop. The shearers didn't think much of our wool clip either. Their job was over and done with far quicker than usual and they moved on to the next farm.

Towards the middle of the month, Ruth asked me if I could come to her house for Sunday dinner. Mother agreed. I rode Star to church that Sunday and then followed the Henschke buggy back along the Track with little Fred up behind me on the horse. Ruth had Harry up with her. He was only six. The rest of the family were all packed into the buggy, sitting on each other's knees, laughing and talking all the way home.

I always liked going to the Henschkes' farm. It was somehow different from ours. They had about the same number of sheep and cows as we did but they were trying out a few pigs as well. Dad was always saying he might give pigs a go too if Mr Henschke's were successful. More surprising than the pigs were the vines. No one else in the valley had ever tried to grow grapes but the Henschkes had had about twenty rows of them for a good long while. The first lot that Mr Henschke's father had planted had been wiped out by some disease but then they'd put in some new ones. A better strain, Mr Henschke said. They didn't ever sell the grapes. I don't think there would have been much of a market for them in those days though there would be now. The valley is full of vines today. The Henschkes just made their own wine from the grapes and stowed it away in a cold cellar that they'd dug out right under the house. They drank it on Sundays and on birthdays. They certainly had a lot of birthdays in that family and they made a bigger fuss about every single one of them than we ever did. Mother and Dad had both been given a glass of wine each year when they went in for Mrs Henschke's birthday but they didn't really like it much. Dad always said, afterwards at home, that beer was a far better drink. Mother liked her own lemonade best. But they always sipped away politely at the Henschkes' white wine and said how cool and delicious it was. Mr Henschke knew how to make the stuff. He'd learnt it from his father and he'd taught Martin and Hans. The whole family just regarded wine-making as one of the normal farming jobs though it always seemed a bit strange to me. We were very impressed all the same. Wine-making was something different. Something interesting.

The Henschkes' garden was rather different too. It was far bigger than ours and lay on all four sides of the house. They had flowers in the front and vegetables at the back, just as we did, but they had far more than us in the way of fruit. In fact they had an orchard. Everyone in the valley had a couple of lemon trees near the back door of the house and a few walnuts and apple trees. But the Henschkes had thick rows of apples and walnuts. They had peaches and plums and apricots. I loved that place in blossom time. They grew blackcurrants and redcurrants, gooseberries and raspberries and even strawberries. Mrs Henschke was a great one for bottling and jam-making. All the women in the valley liked to do those jobs and there was even a bit of rivalry at Show time to see who had the best jams and the most perfectly bottled plums. Mrs Henschke wasn't really a better bottler than the other women but she simply had far more fruit than anyone else so she had more glowing bottles of red and golden fruit standing in rows in her pantry and more jars of jam on her shelves. She was generous with it too and often gave Mother her jam to try. She was always willing to give a few bottles for the church fête or the school bazaar. And nothing went to waste. Not with that big family. By the end of the winter everything had been eaten and Mrs Henschke was ready to start laying in her stocks of sugar for the next season's bottling and jam-making.

The Henschkes had a special herb garden. Thyme and marjoram and mint, of course, like everyone else, but lots of other herbs too that were supposed to be good for various illnesses. That family was very interested in illness. They were all fairly healthy on the whole. We were too. The doctor at Wally was so far off that we couldn't really afford to get sick. But what Mrs Henschke enjoyed was just talking about illness and about the wonderful remedies she had in the herb garden — remedies for constipation and for headaches and for sleeplessness. She knew how to make funny-tasting teas out of all sorts of leaves, even leaves from the wild trees in the bush, and her children would drink them up obediently whenever they felt the slightest bit sick. I was inclined to laugh at Mrs Henschke's magic teas but Ruth wouldn't let me laugh. It was a serious subject as far as she was concerned and not to be laughed at at all.

Mrs Henschke herself and Margaret did all the gardening. That's where they were different from the rest of us. In our family and on most of the valley farms, the women grew the flowers and the men grew the vegetables and fruit. It was a kind of unwritten law that everyone knew about. Everyone except the Henschkes. Mr Henschke never touched the garden at all though he looked after the orchard and the vines. The garden was Mrs Henschke's own kingdom. She and Margaret got up early to work there before the day was too hot and they were at it again in the cool of the evening — hoeing, digging, weeding, raking, planting, picking, pruning, and carrying bucket after bucket of water from their creek. It was an endless job, winter and summer, but they loved it. Whenever Dad and Mother dropped in for a cup of tea or the annual glass of wine, the first thing they had to do was to 'see the garden'. We didn't ever show anyone our garden. It was quite nice and anyone who wanted to look at it was welcome but our attitude to it was utterly different. Our garden was just there by the house, pleasant and useful. But to the Henschkes, their garden was a continual source of pride and joy. We'd learnt not just to walk through it in silence but to make the right kind of exclamations as we went and to admire all we saw. We didn't have to pretend. We really did admire it. That garden was a wonder of amazing order and neatness. It was rich with greens and reds and blues. The scent of lavender and rosemary and lily-of-the-valley hung over it. The soft fruit, the berries, were caged in green nets to keep off the marauding birds. There was even a seat to sit on where you could rest and admire the garden flourishing all around you. We had no seat in our garden. Mother just used to dash out and pick a sprig of parsley or mint and dash back into the house again. She didn't ever linger.

Just beyond the back fence of the garden was the wired pen for all Mrs Henschke's poultry. She had ducks and hens in there and a couple of fierce black roosters. The children did the feeding with bran and pollard and they collected the eggs. The 'chooks' those kids called all of them, even the roosters, but Mrs Henschke fondly called them her 'birds'. They were only shut up in the pen at night. In the day time they wandered all over the yard and into the paddocks. But she kept them firmly out of her beloved garden.

There was wine that Sunday when I went back with the Henschkes after church. It was Margaret's birthday. She was nineteen. Mother had given me a cutting from our pink geranium to bring her as a present and Margaret was delighted. She put it up on the mantelpiece with all her other presents. She sat next to her father at the table in the special seat they called the 'birthday seat'. Even with Martin away in the city and Bernie in Wallaceville, there were still ten of the family around the scrubbed wooden table in the kitchen. I made the eleventh. That was the biggest difference between our place and the Henschkes. Now Laurie was gone there were only three at our table — or four with the Schoolie. You can run out of things to talk about in a small family but the Henschkes always had plenty to say to each other. Even the little ones joined in. They began the meal more formally than we did. Dad's grace was amazingly brief by their standards. They all stood behind their chairs while Mr Henschke offered thanks at some length, with different words every time. Then everyone sat down and Mrs Henschke carried the food across from the stove and put it on the table. She served up the eleven platefuls and Ruth passed the vegetables. You couldn't start till everyone had been served. Then Mrs Henschke said 'Good appetite!' and we all began to eat.

Where we had roasts on Sundays, they had stews. But not ordinary old stews. Mrs Henschke's stews were thick with dumplings as well as meat. The herbs she put in made them taste quite different from ours. Mr Henschke filled the wine glasses — even mine. Only Fred and Harry and Tom had water. I wasn't sure if Mother would really like me to drink wine but I didn't want to say I was too young. It was the first time I'd been given any and I felt very pleased with myself. Mr Henschke must think I was old enough now. I wondered if it was because I helped Dad on the farm but then I saw that Lisa and Kate had as much as I did so it couldn't have been that.

"To Margaret! The birthday girl!" said Mr Henschke, raising his glass.

"Margaret!" we all murmured and raised our glasses and sipped. The wine tasted strange but nice. I couldn't help feeling that Margaret was far too old to be called a 'birthday girl' but, as I told you, they always made a great fuss about birthdays. Mrs Henschke not only told everyone at Deepwater when her birthday came round but exactly how old she was too! Mother said that was rather odd. The women in our valley didn't like people to know their age. They didn't want to grow old but the Henschkes seemed to be prouder the older they grew!

Just above Mrs Henschke's head, on the wall next to the stove, I caught sight of a picture I'd never seen there before. It was the King and the Queen, all dressed up in their coronation robes, with crowns on their heads. Round the edge was a wide frame painted in shiny gold.

I nudged Ruth.

"You've got a new picture," I said with interest. "Where did it come from?"

Mrs Henschke answered me.

"It was the man at the door, Char. Haven't you got one too?"

I shook my head.

"We've only got an old picture of Grandma on her wedding day," I said.

"There was a hawker round last week," said Mrs Henschke. "Such a nice young man, too. Not like the one that brings the salt. He had a good white horse and the pictures were in the saddle-bags. He told me everyone in the valley was buying one of these pictures. Because of the war, he said. To show we're loyal. I thought your mother would've bought one, Char."

"I don't think he came to us," I said and then wished I hadn't. Mrs Henschke looked sad.

"It cost a lot too," she said. "And the frame was more still. But I didn't like to say no. It didn't seem loyal. He said he'd just sold one at the school."

"Yep," said Fred. "Miss Playfair bought one. She said everyone ought to have one. Hers is smaller than this, though."

It certainly was enormous.

"He didn't show me any other sizes," said Mrs Henschke.

"Don't worry, Katherine," said Mr Henschke who'd been

48

looking across at her. "The picture's a minor problem. I'm glad we've got it. Now everyone'll know that we're loyal to the King. The real question is what we're going to do about the children. I don't think they can stand that school much longer. It's all getting out of hand."

"What's wrong?" I asked. "I thought Dad put a stop to all that. He went and talked to the kids."

Mr Henschke tipped back in his chair and put down his fork. He was a big handsome man, his fair hair just starting to turn grey.

"Didn't Ruth tell you?" he asked. "The children in that school have stopped shouting out those awful words, all right. But now they don't speak at all. No one says a word to Ruth or the other four."

"They just turn their backs on us," said Kate.

"And they hold their noses, too," said Fred, "as if we stink!"

"But what does Miss Playfair do about it?" I asked indignantly.

"Nothing," said Ruth.

"Have you told her?"

Ruth shook her head.

"What's the point? She must know. She just does nothing."

"That Miss Playfair started it all!" said Lisa, glowering across the table. "I don't know how you can have her in your house, Charlotte Ross!"

I sprang to Miss Playfair's defence without thinking.

"But she's so nice and kind, really," I said. "And her father sends her all the news about the war every week. He reads two papers a day, you see, cover to cover. And she lets me help her make the little flags. For her map." My voice faltered. I didn't like to go on to tell them how she glided along the floor and how wonderfully her hair was coiled up on top of her head.

"I'm sure she's a good young woman," said Mr Henschke. "But she's set off something ugly in that school. Not on purpose, mind. Just without knowing what she was doing."

"I don't see that we can do anything about it, Dan," said Mrs Henschke. "Kids are always cruel. It can't be helped. Lisa and Kate and Fred and Harry will just have to put up with it. Ruth's only got a few weeks to go till the end of the year. Surely she can stick it out."

"I can't!" said Ruth.

"Who's the leader?" I asked. "Who starts all this not-speaking?"

"The Pollocks," said Ruth. "Sid and Annie. They're the ones behind it. But all the others join in."

"I must admit I've found Mr Pollock rather off-hand in the store lately," said Mrs Henschke. "He's always saying he's run out of this and run out of that because of the war. He even says he can't get sugar now. How can we do the bottling without sugar?"

"Bottle in plain water, Katherine," said Mr Henschke. "It's just as good."

Mrs Henschke sighed.

"There's not much of that left either!" she said.

"I suppose we just might have to go all the way into Wally to stock up with food if Pollock gets any worse about selling us things," said Mr Henschke. "But I can't quite believe that he'd be so mean. He's always been a decent bloke. You might be imagining all that, Katherine."

"But Dad," said Ruth. "What about the kids at school? That's much worse than the sugar. Why should those Pollocks pick on us? Why does the whole school gang up on us?"

"Let's face it, Ruth," said her father. "The plain fact is that we do have a German name. My father did come from Germany. We've always been proud of it. He used to draw me a map to show me the very town where he was born. That was when I was a kid at the school here myself. No one's ever minded that we have a German name. Father arrived in the valley along with all the Scots and there's never been a word of trouble till now. What the Pollocks don't seem to realize is that, although our name is German, we're just as Australian as everyone else. We don't speak German. We can't even read it. German's a foreign language to us, even though I used to hear my parents talking it to each other years ago. They always used English with us. They wanted us to fit in."

"Well, we don't fit in any more!" said Ruth.

"Miss Playfair says the war'll be over by Christmas," I said. "Then everything'll be back to normal again."

"Miss Playfair could be wrong!" said Hans bluntly.

Hans never said much but when he did we all listened. He was eighteen, just like our Laurie, and he'd been working on the farm with his father for four years. He looked very like Martin and Mr Henschke — big and fair and gentle — but he had a tougher streak in him. I stared at him. I was shocked at the very idea that Miss Playfair could be wrong. Such an awful thought had never occurred to me before.

"She's very clever," I said lamely.

"Let's leave Miss Playfair out of this," said Mr Henschke firmly. "She's only a girl. Not much older than Margaret here. I'm sure she meant no harm. I'll go and tackle Don Pollock himself. I'll tell him what his kids are up to at the school. I've known the man for forty years, after all! He'll give them a good talking-to and maybe all this trouble'll blow over."

I wasn't so sure myself. I hoped he was right.

"What about the puppets, Dad?" asked Fred. "Couldn't we have them out just for the family at Christmas? And for Char's family? No one else would ever know."

Mr Henschke shook his head.

"The puppets have been put away till the war's over."

"Where?" asked Kate.

"Never mind where they are. I'm telling no one at all. Not even your mother."

"Is the Bible there too, Dan?" asked Mrs Henschke, frowning with worry.

Mr Henschke looked startled.

"I forgot all about the Bible!" he said.

"There's nothing wrong with having a Bible, Mrs Henschke," I said. "Everyone's got one."

"This is a German Bible, Char," she said. "Ruth's grandfather brought it out with him from Germany. We've written all the births and marriages and deaths in the front."

"Do you mean the people in Germany have the same Bible as us?" I asked in astonishment.

"Of course they do!" said Hans sharply. "Only it's all

51

written in German instead of English. The words mean the same."

"Could I see it? I won't tell Miss Playfair you've got it."

Mr Henschke hesitated a minute and looked across at his wife. She nodded and he went into the front room to bring the Bible. It was a huge heavy book, far bigger than ours, and bound in thick black leather with gold lettering on the cover. He laid it down carefully at his end of the table.

"Come and see, Char," he said to me.

I left my seat next to Ruth and walked down behind all the chairs to stand beside Mr Henschke. I looked at the book. 'Die Bibel', it said on the front. He opened it up and turned the pages so I could see the strange printing set out in long columns, just like our Bible at home. I couldn't read a word of it! He turned back to the pages where the family events were written.

"There's Ruth's birth," he said, "with Bernie's. The turn of the century. 1900. Those were the last ones my father wrote in before he died. I had to take over then. Martin will have the Bible when I'm gone."

He broke off suddenly. I thought of Martin, heading for the war. I suppose everyone was thinking of Martin just then. Martin Brown! Would he ever want the German Bible?

"Put it away, dear," said Mrs Henschke. "It can go with the puppets, wherever they are. There's nothing else from Germany in the house so we won't need to worry."

"There's the violin!" said Hans. "You mustn't hide that away, Dad. We can do without the puppets and the Bible for a while but you can't manage without your violin. Anyway, I want to play it too."

"Lots of people have German violins, surely," said Mrs Henschke.

"We could scratch the name off," suggested Ruth.

"We'll see," said Mr Henschke. He closed up the Bible slowly and took it out of the room.

"Dishes!" said Mrs Henschke briskly. "Come on girls."

Margaret, Ruth, Lisa and Kate began to clear the table. I helped them. Hans and Fred and the two little boys ran out into the afternoon sun. I didn't see Mr Henschke again but when I set out to ride home I heard the sound of his violin coming from the front room. The tune he played was slow and sad.

Back home, Miss Playfair had the latest newspaper cuttings from her father spread out on the kitchen table. She was reading them carefully and marking some columns with her red pencil. Then she cut them out with Mother's old scissors and pasted them into a scrap book. That was her 'War Book'. She took it down to the school with her every day to keep the kids up to date and she let me read it in the evenings. Somehow I didn't feel like reading it that night. I sat opposite her at the table, saying nothing, and wondering where Mr Henschke had hidden his puppets. I didn't care so much about the Bible but I hated to think of those lovely bright puppets, taken off their hooks on the wall of the front room and shoved away in the barn or in the cellar. Their clothes would get all crushed. They wouldn't be able to see in the dark.

I don't know if Mr Henschke did have that talk with Mr Pollock at the store or not. I suppose he did. But only a few days later, something happened that drove all thought of the kids' nasty silence at the school right out of my mind. Mrs Henschke was back in our kitchen crying again. Mother didn't send me out this time. She just pointed to a chair so I sat down and listened.

The Henschkes had had a visit that afternoon from Mr McDonald. He'd ridden the whole way out from Wally to see them. He'd brought bad news. Bernie had gone! Disappeared! He hadn't turned up for work that morning — it was a Wednesday, I remember — and the family where he boarded had found his bed unslept in. A few clothes had gone too and some bread from the kitchen and an old black billy from the shed.

"But why?" Mother asked. "I thought he liked that job with Mr McDonald."

"He did!" sobbed Mrs Henschke.

I hated seeing grown-ups cry. Their faces collapsed

somehow and went all creased. It made me feel embarrassed. So I tried desperately to think of something cheerful that might stop her.

"He could've joined up, Mrs Henschke, and gone off to the war. Just like Laurie and Martin."

Mrs Henschke cried louder still.

"He's far too young, Char," said Mother. "He's only fourteen after all. I know he's a big boy for his age but he'd never persuade anyone that he's eighteen. No, that can't be it. Mrs Henschke, he must have gone to visit some of your relations. That's where he'll be."

Mother always said 'Mrs Henschke'. Mrs Henschke always called Mother 'Mrs Ross'. They'd known each other well for twenty years but they didn't call each other 'Katherine' or 'Emily'. It wasn't the custom in those days.

Mrs Henschke dried her tears now and pulled herself together. Mother made a pot of tea and took some oatcakes out of a large glass jar. She poured the tea.

"Now where is it that those sisters of yours live, Mrs Henschke?" she asked.

"Swan Hill. Up on the Murray. But Bernie wouldn't go up there. I'm sure of it. My sisters are rather strict, Mrs Ross. They've never got on well with any of our children. They're not married themselves, you see, so they're not used to children. When they came down to stay with us for a week or so last year, they told me straight out that they thought I was far too lax with the boys. They didn't seem to mind the girls so much. And they said Bernie was rude to them though I'm sure he never meant to be. He didn't like them one bit. He'd never go up there. Anyway, he had no money for a train fare and it's too far too walk."

"Well, what about Mr Henschke? Hasn't he got any relations?"

Mrs Henschke shook her head.

"But *why* did he leave?" I asked. That seemed to me more important than speculating on where he could have gone.

"Mr McDonald says it's all to do with the war," said Mrs Henschke. "There's been bad feeling building up in

Wallaceville ever since August. Anyone with a German name's in trouble. That nice Mr Goldschmidt who had the lolly shop on the corner of Barnes Street has had to shut down his business. He's left the town. And they've changed Berlin Street to Birmingham Street. But it's much worse than that. Mr McDonald had stones flying through the window of his workshop one night last week. And he's had a couple of nasty letters too. Unsigned letters, of course. They said he was a traitor to his country, having a German as an apprentice. He didn't say a word to Bernie about them. He just ripped them up and threw them away. But I can't help wondering if Bernie had any letters like that himself."

"Perhaps the family where he was living have caught this silly German fever," said Mother. "Who are they, again?"

"The Locheads in Philip Street. They're nice enough people. I don't think they'd be like that at all. Dan's ridden back into town with Mr McDonald now. He's going to the police station and then he'll see the Locheads."

"They might know something," said Mother. "Have some more tea, Mrs Henschke."

I slipped out of the room and left them talking. I went to the barn where it was cool and sat on a bale of straw, thinking about Bernie. What could have happened to him? Why had he gone? Where could he run to? I found no answers at all. Then Dad called me and I came out into the hot afternoon sun again. Two more of our ewes were panting on the ground. Dying probably. I helped Dad load each one into a wheelbarrow and take it into the shade. I brought water in a bucket from the river. As we worked, I could see Mrs Henschke on her way home again, walking slowly down to our farm gate with Mother beside her. I told Dad that Bernie had gone. Disappeared.

When Miss Playfair came in from school, later that afternoon, Mother and I didn't say a word to her about Bernie's disappearance. Somehow we both felt that the less said the better. Miss Playfair had plenty to talk about anyway so our awkward silence over tea wasn't noticed at all. Her Pageant about the Empire was going well. The mothers were making costumes out of sheets and cardboard. Miss Playfair's father was even sending one or two special costumes up from the city. All she needed now, she said, was some music. I didn't suggest Mr Henschke's violin. I told her about Mr Logan's bagpipes. She was delighted with the idea.

"I'll give a note to Jeff or Molly tomorrow. Do you think he'd be willing to come and play for the Pageant, Mrs Ross? Just at the beginning and the end?"

"I think so," said Mother, not really paying much attention to the Schoolie. Her mind was on other things that evening. She turned to me.

"You can go down and see Ruth tonight, Char," she said. "After we've had tea. I've made a quick batch of shortbread for Mrs Henschke. You could take them along for me."

I was quite glad of an excuse to escape from the War Book and the little black flags. I wanted to see Ruth. I had a fair idea of the state she'd be in if she knew Bernie had gone.

What exactly was it about Ruth and Bernie? Twins are not always close to each other, I suppose, especially when they're not identical, but Ruth and Bernie had always seemed to me like the two halves of one person. When they were younger they'd even looked quite alike — the same startlingly blue eyes, the same gestures, the same springy walk, the same hair that was so fair it was almost white. Lately they'd both begun to change. Bernie had suddenly grown taller and thinner. Bonier. Ruth had become plumper. Not fat. Just comfortable-looking. But even back in their early days, it had never been their similar appearance that was so striking. It was the way their minds worked.

The three of us had started school together in the middle of the year that we all turned five. I sat next to Ruth in the front desk and Bernie sat by himself in the desk on her other side. We were the only ones in that grade and all the grades were in the same room. We began with the letters of the alphabet — little a, big A, little b, big B — and over the years we went on bit by bit to proper reading and writing and to sums and to singing our tables just like the older ones. The two big kids in the desk at the very back of the room did look enormous to us in our first year. They used to come and help us with our work. They'd squash into the desk beside us to show us how to make our letters and our numbers. Ruth and Bernie and I used to wonder if we'd ever get to sitting in the big desk at the back. And of course we did in the end. Ruth and I were still together and Bernie in the seat beside us. We used to help the little ones in our turn.

Bernie was the best teacher of the three of us. The five-year-olds always wanted him to come and sit beside them. He knew how to give them confidence. He used to make up funny little games and rhymes to help them remember their spelling. Mr Edwards was pleased with all of us when we were in Grade 7 and Grade 8 but he was proudest of Bernie. Bernie was his prize pupil — quick with mental arithmetic, neat in his handwriting, good with a football or a cricket bat out in the yard at playtime, fast as an eel in the water of Mr Craik's dam when we all plunged into it on hot afternoons in the years before the drought. Mr Edwards was quite upset when Bernie left school the day he turned fourteen and went off to be the carpenter's apprentice. He'd had great plans for Bernie. He wanted to put him in for a scholarship at a high school down in the city. But Bernie was definite. He'd had enough of school. He wanted to work. He wanted to be a carpenter and he thought he was lucky to get the apprenticeship with Mr McDonald when four or five other boys in Wally were after it.

In all those years, from the 'Bubs' (as we used to say) up to the start of Grade 8, as the three of us had worked our way up the school together and moved from the front desks to the back, I'd become aware of the strangely close bond between Bernie and Ruth. In the playground, of course, he mainly played with the boys unless they needed all the girls to join in to make up a team. But inside the school room and on the way home along Gillespie's Track, they were always together — with me hanging on as a kind of extra, sometimes between them, sometimes on one side or the other. When they were still little, if one of them fell over and started to cry, the other would soon be crying too. When they were a bit older, if Mr Edwards praised Bernie, Ruth would beam with pride. They quarrelled with all their other brothers and sisters from time to time, just as everyone does in families, but they didn't ever quarrel with each other. They didn't actually talk to each other much. I'm afraid I was the one that did most of the talking. But they each seemed to know perfectly well what the other was thinking. Occasionally they'd even start to say the same thing at the same moment in exactly the same words. Then they'd look at each other and laugh. Sometimes I felt a bit jealous. I wanted to be the one that was closest to Ruth. But I came to see that I just couldn't compete with Bernie. The bond between them wasn't quite what I'd call love. It was simply that they seemed to be part of each other.

Once Bernie had left school in April and moved into Wally, Ruth didn't seem her old self any more. She drooped, somehow. She talked about Bernie a lot in the first few months. It was always 'Bernie this' and 'Bernie that' till I was almost sick and tired of hearing his name. But then he gradually dropped out of her conversation. She didn't ever quite recover her old high spirits. She seemed to be living at half pressure all the time. When she stayed on at the school after I left in August, she was the only one there to teach the little ones but her heart wasn't in it any longer. She told me she wanted to leave and get some kind of a job in Wally itself. Working for a dressmaker, she said. Then she'd be near Bernie. But Mr Henschke wouldn't consider that for a minute. His daughter wasn't going to have to work.

"You'll stay here and help your mother, Ruth," he used to say to her kindly whenever she brought the matter up. I often heard him. "I know you miss Bernie. That's only natural. We all miss him. But he has to make his way in the world and your place is here at home. This farm can't support all the boys but it can support you till the day you get married. Then someone else will look after you."

Ruth used to sigh. I don't think her father ever grasped just how much she missed Bernie.

So now that Bernie had disappeared or run away or whatever he had done, I knew she would be frantic. She was too. When I reached their house with the plate of shortbread in my hand that evening, she was lying on her bed and crying like a child. There were two iron bedsteads in the girls' room. Ruth shared one of them with Margaret. Now she was sprawled right out across the blue quilt, her black boots still on her feet. She was stuffing her pillow into her mouth to stifle the sobs.

I sat on the bed beside her.

"Please stop, Ruth," I said but she hardly seemed to hear me. I didn't know what to say. I sat there silent for half an hour. In the end I just had to leave her and go back home. I knew I wasn't any use. I couldn't break through to her at all.

It was about a mile from the Henschkes' place to ours. Down their little track and past their dried-up dam to the farm gate; then out onto Gillespie's Track for half a mile or so to our gate; then up beside the dusty bed of our creek to the house. I ran the whole way that night. The stars were brilliant. They're always like that in the valley. I was dying to tell Mother about Ruth and how helpless I'd felt sitting there beside her. But when I burst into the kitchen I knew at once that my worries would have to wait. Miss Playfair was there, pasting some more news into her War Book at the table, and Mr Mallorie had just arrived. Mother was offering him some of our left-over stew but for once he didn't want it.

"No thanks, Mrs Ross," he said, lowering himself carefully onto an upright kitchen chair. "I've eaten plenty already. Good corned beef. Solid stuff, that. No. I've jist brought me stone down to show the Schoolie here."

He fished about first in one trouser pocket and then in the other.

"Here it is! Now, Miss, what d'you think of that?"

He slapped his stone down on the open War Book and tipped back in his chair.

Miss Playfair picked up the stone. Dad leaned forward from his end of the table; Mother came closer and I stood beside her. We all stared at the strange stone as Miss Playfair turned it round and round in her fingers. It was hand-sized and more than filled her small palm. It was smooth and grey, all rounded at the ends and with a notch where the fingers could grip it at one side. Its surface was pitted all over with thousands of tiny sickle-shaped scratches. Right in the centre was an oval hole, divided inside into two chambers. The chamber on the left came to a sudden flinty end — you could just fit a thumb into it. The other chamber went right through to the other side of the stone. Stuck in this hole was a dark orange pebble that almost filled the space. Miss Playfair passed the stone to me. It felt surprisingly heavy in my hand. I put one finger in the hole and pressed against the pebble. It didn't move. I turned the stone over and pushed on the pebble from the other side where it was nearer the surface. Again it didn't move. Dad took the stone and then Mother.

"How did that pebble get in there?" she asked, jabbing at it hard with her finger.

"Goodness knows," said Dad. "Maybe the sea pushed it in there — or a river. Do you have any idea where it came from, Keith? That chap who gave it to you — had he picked it up himself?"

"Don't know," said Mr Mallorie. "He didn't never say much about it. You don't find no stones like that at Eaglehawk. It's the wrong kind of stone. Not quartz, is it, Alec?"

Dad shook his head.

"Not from gold country," he said, "and not from the hills round here either. It's a mystery all right. Looks like a sea-stone to me. Someone could've found it on a beach somewhere."

"Stones with holes right through the middle are supposed to be lucky," said Mr Mallorie. "That's what me old Dad always reckoned. He said I oughter hang it up outside. Over the door or the winder. It'd keep out the witches, he said. Can't say I've been bothered with witches so I've never tried it."

Miss Playfair had the stone again now. She passed it from her left hand to her right hand and back again.

"Robert Somerville Playfair!" said Mr Mallorie. "That's the bloke that give it to me. Best present I ever had. Never seen another one like it."

"Perhaps it's a kind of family heirloom," said Mother. "It's funny that Mr Playfair ever gave it away."

"He wasn't married in them days," said Mr Mallorie. "He was well over forty, mind. He'd been married, me Dad said, but the poor wife'd died on the diggings. He got married again later — or so we heard. After he'd given up the diggings and gone south. So he didn't have no family to give the stone to — not when I knew him."

"You could leave it to Miss Playfair in your will, Mr Mallorie," I suggested. "Then it'd come back into the right family."

Mother looked quite shocked at this idea of mine. Wills suggested death and that was something she didn't like mentioned.

"Never made a will," said Mr Mallorie. "P'raps I should. Nothink much to leave. Only the old hut. Who'd want that? How d'you go about making a will, Alec?"

"You're supposed to go and see the lawyer in Wally. You know the bloke — Bert Bradley in Berlin Street. Birmingham Street, I mean. He writes it all out properly and then you sign it. Mind you, he doesn't do it for nothing. You have to pay him. I suppose you could just write it out yourself. But you need to have someone to sign it with you. A witness."

"Terrible lot of bother," muttered Mr Mallorie. "Still, I wouldn't want me stone chucked out on the hill when I'm dead and gone. Someone oughter have it. What d'you think, Miss? D'you want to have me old stone — when I'm gone?"

Miss Playfair went red. I don't think she liked all this talk of death and wills any more than Mother did. I had a feeling she didn't care for the stone much either.

"I *would* like it," she said slowly. "Because of my grandfather. But isn't there someone else in your family that should have it, Mr Mallorie?"

"No family," he said. "No wife, no kids, no worries, nothink. Jist the hut and me stone."

I couldn't help remembering those stories of the money under his mattress. Surely he must have had some cash left from the sale of his land, but perhaps it had all gone already on tins of corned beef.

"You could leave your hut to the church," suggested

Mother. "Then they could sell off your little bit of land and buy a nice carpet or something."

Mr Mallorie snorted. He wasn't ever one for the church. Never went near the place. He reached out and took the stone back from Miss Playfair.

I wished *I* could inherit the stone. I loved the feel of it. I was sure it would bring me good luck. Still, Miss Playfair had more right to it than I did — if it was true that her grandfather had really owned it once. Robert Somerville Playfair.

"Try hanging it up, Mr Mallorie," I said. "See what happens. You could just get a bit of string past that pebble."

Mr Mallorie smiled to himself and slid the stone back into the depths of his pocket. He got to his feet and pulled on his sagging trousers, bending stiffly to hitch at them just above the knee.

"How's that war getting on?" he asked with a nod towards Miss Playfair's book.

She looked anxious.

"Not very well," she said. "My father thought it would all be over by Christmas but I'm not so sure now. I'm going to need more black flags."

Mother and Dad looked at each other down the table. I was thinking of Laurie too.

"I been thinking," Mr Mallorie went on. "I reckon I'd like to help."

Miss Playfair was surprised.

"Making flags, do you mean? But Charlotte here is a great help. I don't think I need as many as all that."

"No. Not flags. Knitting. You give me the wool. I've got plenty of needles up in me hut. I'll knit you a scarf for the soldiers."

Miss Playfair laughed.

"I mean it!" said Mr Mallorie sharply. "I'm a damned good knitter. Me mother taught me. You jist get me the wool. You'll see what I can do."

Miss Playfair looked at Mother in bewilderment.

"It's true," said Mother. "Old Mrs Mallorie was the finest knitter in the whole valley. Mr Mallorie here could knit better than any of the women. I've seen his work. He made his old mother a beautiful shawl."

"But I'm not sure . . ." said Miss Playfair uncertainly. "The scarves all have to follow the same pattern, you see."

"That's all right", said Mr Mallorie. "Give me the wool and tell me the pattern. Where do you keep that khaki stuff? Here in the house? I could take it now."

"No. It's all down at the school."

"Righto. I'll come and get it tomorrer."

He moved slowly to the door.

"I'll make a cup of tea, Mr Mallorie," said Mother. "The kettle's always on the boil. Stay and have one with us."

"No thanks," he said. "I'll be getting on up the hill. See you tomorrer, Miss."

"I'll walk a bit of the way with you, Keith," said Dad and followed Mr Mallorie out of the back door.

I knew why Dad wanted to go with him. He'd be telling him all about Bernie. I don't really know why we didn't want to talk about Bernie's disappearance in front of Miss Playfair. Somehow, we didn't.

5. White Feathers

"Charlotte," said Miss Playfair, as we sat around the table having tea the next evening. "Ruth Henschke wasn't at school today. Is she sick or something?"

"I'm not sure," I said, glancing at Mother.

"She isn't very well," said Mother quickly. "Mrs Henschke was telling me about it this morning. I expect she'll be back in a day or two. What about the other Henschkes? Were they at school?"

"Yes. They were all there. A bit quiet, I thought. I do hope it's not catching — whatever it is that Ruth's got. We don't want it running through the school."

"It's probably just the heat," said Mother and changed the subject. "Did Mr Mallorie come to collect his wool today?"

"Yes, he was there at nine this morning. He did seem to grasp the pattern quickly but I wasn't sure if it was right to let him have the wool. We can't afford to waste it."

"You don't need to worry about that," said Mother. "He'll knit you a good scarf. He won't waste the wool."

"It does seem strange," said Miss Playfair, frowning. I thought she looked just as beautiful when she frowned as when she smiled. Mostly she didn't do either. She just looked calm and serious. Her face was as smooth as her coiled black hair.

When the table was cleared and the dishes done, Miss Playfair asked me if I could come to her room for a few minutes. I hadn't been in there since the day she'd arrived. My heart leapt with hope. Perhaps she was going to lend me some books or show me her locket. The room was as neat as the day Mother and I had made it ready for her. There were a few books on the little desk and a photograph of a stern bearded man on the dressing-table. He looked quite old — not young — so I decided it was more likely to be her father than a sweetheart.

"Charlotte," she said, sitting on one of the two hard chairs and pointing me to the other, "I need your help."

I glowed with happiness. She needed my help. For the moment, I'd forgotten all about the Henschkes' puppets and the battle over the knitting. I smoothed down my cotton skirt with both hands. I sat up straighter and tried to look wise. But her next question startled me.

"Do you know all the older boys in the families that live round here? The boys who've left school, I mean."

I had an awful suspicion that she might be probing to find out about Bernie. He was an older boy. He'd left school. Could she possibly know he'd run off? No — of course she couldn't. But why would she want to know about the older boys? I tried to sound unconcerned.

"Oh yes, Miss Playfair," I said. "I know them all. Which families do you mean, exactly?"

"Well, the Logans, for example, and the Douglases and the Craiks. Have they any older boys at home?"

I rushed to answer her now that I knew it wasn't Bernie she had in mind.

"I can tell you all about them. Would you like me to write down their names?"

"That's a good idea," she said and passed me a sheet of clean white paper and a neatly sharpened pencil. Miss Playfair always had a good supply of sharpened pencils.

Then, as I took the pencil and spread the paper on her desk, a quite crazy idea came into my head. Suddenly I was sure I knew why she wanted these names. She must be looking for someone to marry! Lady teachers did often marry farmers' sons. I'd heard that. There wasn't any other choice in the country. I was excited at the very thought of it. I could tell her which boys were the nicest and the best-looking and then perhaps she'd marry one of them and she'd settle in our valley for ever. She'd be a neighbour instead of a Schoolie. The war would soon be over and she'd be my best friend. She'd probably even call her first daughter Charlotte — after me. My mind raced ahead with wonderful possibilities. I chewed on the end of my pencil and began.

"Well," I said slowly. "There's Gordon Craik. He's very tall. But I'm afraid he's not here at Deepwater any more. He's gone off to the war."

"Write him down," said Miss Playfair promptly.

I wrote his name but it seemed pointless to me. He couldn't marry her if he wasn't here. It would be far better to stick to the ones she could actually meet.

"Put a W by his name," she said. "Then I'll know he's gone to the war. How old is he?"

"About twenty, I think. Then there's his brother, Bill. But he's only eighteen. He helps Mr Craik on the farm."

"Write him down," said Miss Playfair.

I was pretty sure that Bill Craik was too young to be a husband but I wrote him down.

"There are two big boys in the Morison family," I went on. "Jim's fifteen and Dave's fourteen. They're both on the farm."

I was relieved when she shook her head. She could hardly marry a boy of fourteen!

"Too young," she said. "Don't bother about them. Who else is there?"

"Col Douglas is twenty-two. But he's gone to the war."

"Put him down. Mark him with a W like the other one."

I did as she said.

"Ronnie Douglas is about twenty, I think, and Stu's sixteen."

"Put Ronnie down."

"I don't like Ronnie Douglas much," I said. "He's too pleased with himself."

"That doesn't matter at all, Charlotte," she said. "What does he do?"

"Works on the farm," I said. "Now the Pollocks at the store. They've got Donny. He helps in the shop. He's fifteen. He's got funny eyes."

"Don't bother with him," she said.

66

"Martin Henschke's gone to the war. Hans is eighteen and Bernie's fourteen." I tried to keep my voice flat and calm.

"You can write Martin down. With a W, of course. And put Hans down too."

She showed no interest at all in Bernie. I was thankful for that. Much as I liked the idea of her settling in the valley, she couldn't go marrying Bernie. That would be ridiculous.

"You'd better put your brother down too. With a W."

I added Laurie's name to the list. Could she marry Laurie, I wondered? She'd be my sister!

"How many is that now, Charlotte?" Miss Playfair asked me.

I counted them.

"Four away at the war and three at home," I said. I paused. "The soldiers *could* come back on leave, you know," I added.

"So they could," she said and took my piece of paper and studied the names.

I wondered if I should give her some definite advice. After all, I knew all those boys and she didn't.

"Gordon Craik's probably the best of the bunch," I said slowly, looking down at my hands so as not to catch her eye.

"Thank you, Charlotte. You've been a great help to me." She folded up the paper carefully. "Now I'll just paste a few cuttings into my book. There's some good news this week."

We moved back to the kitchen. Soon we were both busy with scissors and paste. I just couldn't resist helping her. I seemed to be under her spell. I tried not to think about the troubles at the school and I tried not to think about Bernie. I caught myself wondering if Miss Playfair would actually write a letter to Gordon Craik and propose to him. But that wouldn't be very lady-like and she was certainly a lady. Perhaps she would knit him a scarf and slip a little note in with it. "Looking forward to meeting you when you come home." That would be all right, I thought. Not too bold. I did hope Gordon wouldn't go and get killed before the wedding.

"I need a few more flags, Charlotte," said Miss Playfair, breaking in on my thoughts. "You'd better do me six of each. Just to be on the safe side."

Devotedly, I cut out and coloured the flags. I really had forgotten about Bernie by now. As I rubbed in the black crayon and the red and blue, I was thinking how I might even be a bridesmaid. Miss Playfair left me to finish the flags. She went out into the half light to help Mother feed the chooks. That was the first time she'd offered to do anything on the farm.

Later the same week I came into the kitchen and found Mother sitting and staring out of the window. This was odd. She was never one for sitting about. She was always working and always moving.

"What is it?" I asked her.

"I was thinking about Ruth. I've just been down to the Henschkes. Ruth's not eating."

"Not eating at all! She'll die if she doesn't eat!"

"What I mean is she won't eat proper meals with the family. She just stays in the girls' room. She lies on the bed all day, Mrs Henschke says. But in the middle of the night, when everyone else is asleep, she creeps into the kitchen and helps herself to an apple or a carrot or a bit of bread. They find the crumbs and the cores in the morning. So she won't actually starve to death. But she's getting thinner. It's very peculiar. I think you'd better go down and see her, Char. Mrs Henschke thought you might be able to talk some sense into her."

I went but I had no success. In fact I found it all quite frightening. Ruth was still sprawled across the bed, more or less exactly as I'd seen her before. She was white-faced and dry-eyed. She wouldn't speak to me at all. I plied her with questions but there were no answers. I tried to tell her that Bernie knew perfectly well how to look after himself. I told her the war would be over any day now. I begged her to eat properly. She just stared through me as if I wasn't there at all. She didn't seem to see me or to hear me. I began to feel invisible. In the end I left her and came home again.

"It's no use," I said to Mother. "She won't listen."

"You must keep on going, Char. Try again tomorrow."

"I don't want to!" I muttered angrily.

"You must. No one else can get through to her."

"Neither can I."

"You'll have to try. You're her friend."

"Why doesn't Dad do something to find Bernie? That's all Ruth needs — she's sick because she doesn't know where Bernie is. Nothing else can help her."

"He's doing what he can," said Mother. "He's had a good talk to Mr Henschke to find out where Bernie might have run off to. Not that Mr Henschke had much idea. And he's riding into Wally tomorrow to see the police. He gets the feeling that they're not doing much to find Bernie."

"It's not surprising, is it?"

"What do you mean?"

"German fever! The police have probably got German fever. Like Miss Playfair and Mr Pollock at the store and those kids at the school. The police won't even bother looking for Bernie. They think he's just a German."

"Don't be silly, Char. Bernie's not a German!"

"I know. But the police think he is. They just take one look at his name. They probably think he's a spy."

"Your ideas are running away with you, Char!" said Mother sharply. "You'd better go on outside and help Dad with the work."

I went to look for Dad. I was pretty sure I'd find him at the river. Our own little creek had dried up completely now. The last muddy holes had turned to hard clay. With the tank empty at the back door and the creek dry, our only source of water for the stock was the river. Dad went there every afternoon with his long water-cart — the Furphy, he called it — to fill it up for the cattle and sheep. We didn't actually drink the river water ourselves and I was glad of that. It looked so murky. Mr Mallorie's spring was still flowing well and he'd offered us a few bucketsful a day for our own washing and drinking. We weren't the only ones. All the other farmers at Deepwater trekked up the hill to Mr Mallorie's spring with their clanking buckets. He was keeping the whole settlement in drinking water. He said his spring would never run dry but I wasn't so sure.

The river was no longer the wide raging stream of last year.

You could hardly call it Deepwater any more! It was barely ten paces from one side to the other and only a few inches deep. Dad was standing bare-footed right out in the middle with the water lapping round his ankles. He was pushing the end of the hose well down and trying to fix it in place with a couple of stones.

"Char!" he called out when he saw me. "This blessed hose keeps bobbing up again. You come and hold it under the water for me and I'll pump."

I pulled off my boots and socks and waded in after him. The river water was warm. It hardly moved. I pushed the hose right down and looked across at the thick bush on the far bank.

"I could walk right across, Dad!" I said. "Over to the wild side!"

"Mmm," said Dad, not really listening to me. He was pumping hard.

"How much longer will this river keep running, Dad?" I asked him.

He gazed across the narrow stretch of water.

"Hard to say. Only a month or two if there's no rain. The hills up there are as dry as our paddocks down here. Everyone in the valley's pumping up this water now. It can't last long."

"What'll we do when it's all gone?"

"We'll have to sell off all the stock — or watch them die. We just might have to leave the farm altogether. We can't stay on here when all the water's gone. And we won't be the only ones. Everyone'll be leaving. It'll be nothing but a valley of dry bones!"

Dad always exaggerated when things were bad. I didn't really believe him. But his flat hopeless voice left me feeling troubled.

Ruth wasn't in church with the rest of her family the next Sunday. She must be still on that bed, I thought to myself. The minister prayed for rain. He always did. He preached about the people of Israel wandering in the wilderness and thirsting for water. Moses struck the rock at Horeb and water gushed out. The people drank. We had to trust in God, the minister said. That's what he always said. We sang the last hymn and droned the long Amen after the benediction. The minister came down the steps from his pulpit. We were all just standing up in our places and turning to chat to each other when a sudden loud voice from the back of the church made everyone sit down again.

"Wait a minute!" roared the voice. It was Mr Craik. His big red face was sweating. "There's something I want to say. This is the best place to say it."

The minister scuttled back up to the pulpit, pulling on the black gown again that he'd begun to take off.

"No, Bert!" said Mrs Craik, tugging on her husband's sleeve. "Don't say it! Not in the church! Please!"

"I'm going to say it!" he retorted angrily.

Mrs Craik shrank back in the pew and began to cry soundlessly.

Mr Craik had pulled a brown envelope from his pocket and was holding it high above his head. We all turned round in our seats to stare at him. There was an uncomfortable silence in the church. No one had ever done anything like this before. Was he going to attack the minister, I wondered? Because there hadn't been any rain?

"My son Bill got a letter this week!" shouted Mr Craik. He sounded as if he was addressing a crowd of thousands instead of our tiny little congregation packed into the Kanyul church.

He opened the brown envelope and pushed two fingers inside. He pulled out a soft white feather and waved it in the air.

"This was the letter!" he bellowed. "What does it mean? That's what I want to know? And who's the devil that sent it?"

We all gazed at the waving feather. No one answered his questions. The minister cleared his throat. Then Ronnie Douglas got slowly to his feet. He pulled a white feather from his pocket and held it up.

"I've got one too," he said quietly. "I don't know who sent it. But I know what it means all right."

"What does it mean then?" demanded Mr Craik.

"It means we're cowards. Bill and me. We haven't gone to the war. We've stayed on the farms. Someone thinks we're too scared to fight."

An angry muttering went round the church. Mr Henschke stood up.

"Hans has had the same letter," he said. "The same sort of feather. We thought it was just a joke. I threw it in the fire."

"It's no joke!" said Mr Craik. He was still angry but he seemed relieved that Bill wasn't the only one. "Who else has had these feathers?"

We all looked at each other. No one spoke. Mr Craik went on.

"Well, who sent them? That's what I want to know!"

"What's the postmark?" asked the minister from the pulpit.

We all turned our heads to the front again.

Mr Craik looked at the envelope.

"Deepwater!" he said.

"Someone *here* sent the feathers!" said Mr Henschke. "Someone at Deepwater! Or maybe at Kanyul. Someone in our valley. But let me just tell whoever it is that Hans can't go off to the war! I can't manage the farm without Hans! Martin's gone already. Hans must stay here!"

"And I can't manage without Bill!" said Mr Craik.

Mr Douglas nodded. It was true. He couldn't run his farm without Ronnie either.

But now Bill Craik turned on his father, his eyes blazing.

"You'll just have to manage somehow, Dad! I'm not going to be called a coward by anyone! I'm off to the war tomorrow!"

His father and mother started to argue with him and the same bitter argument was flaring up among the Douglases and the Henschkes. Everyone else in the church started to join in, giving advice over the back of the pew, talking indignantly to anyone who would listen. The younger children were enjoying themselves. Church wasn't usually so interesting.

"The real question is," said the minister, trying to be heard over the hubbub, "who sent these feathers?"

"It doesn't matter who sent them," said Mr Henschke. "We'll never know."

Oh yes we will, I thought to myself! I knew already who it was! I looked sideways at Miss Playfair. She was sitting right next to me. I always managed somehow to get myself next to her in church. She was smiling to herself. She was reading her hymn book. She took no notice of the storm raging around her.

I wanted to denounce her. I wanted to stand up and point my finger at her in front of them all and shout out, "She sent the feathers! Miss Playfair! She asked me for their names and I gave them to her! I didn't know why she wanted them, did I? I thought she was looking for a husband!"

That's what I wanted to say. But in fact I didn't say anything at all. I just sat there, my face burning and hot tears in my eyes. Did Dad know she had sent the letters? Or Mother? They didn't seem to. They were as puzzled as everyone else. But it was all so obvious. I suppose no one could bring himself to suspect a Schoolie. Schoolies were always right. And anyway, Schoolies didn't belong. They were outsiders. Everyone in that church was looking for one who belonged. One of themselves.

"It could be the Pollocks," Dad was saying. "They're not here today."

But Mother shook her head.

The people surged out of church, still arguing and talking. Miss Playfair was very quiet on the way home in the buggy. I was quiet too.

Those three white feathers did their work. Bill Craik and Ronnie Douglas and Hans Henschke all went off to the war the next week. Hans changed his name, of course. To Henderson. Henry Henderson. A bit better than Brown. I suppose, but Mrs Henschke was just as distressed as she'd been about Martin.

"I'm selling up!" said Mr Craik gloomily to Dad the next Sunday. But I wasn't sure if he really meant it.

6. The Travelling Photographer

Once Hans had left the farm to join the army, Mr Henschke was more desperate than ever to find Bernie. They'd all been worried enough about him before. Sometimes Mrs Henschke had even thought he'd been kidnapped or murdered though Mother told her that wasn't likely at all. "No news is good news, Mrs Henschke," she kept saying. But now the Henschkes wanted to find Bernie not just to be sure he was safe and well and not just for Ruth's sake either. They needed him to work on the farm in place of Hans. Mr Henschke never dreamt of letting Margaret or Ruth help on the farm the way I helped Dad. That was unthinkable. They wanted Bernie back again.

Mr Henschke put an advertisement in the Wallaceville weekly paper. It included an old smudgy photograph of Bernie. I could hardly recognize him so I didn't know how other people were going to. Mr Henschke even offered a reward to anyone who could tell him where Bernie had gone or to anyone who had set eyes on him. But no one seemed to have any information. The only answer Mr Henschke got was a rude letter telling him to go back to Hun Land where he belonged and to take all his damned Fritz-kids with him. He brought the letter to show Dad and then he tore it to shreds without a word and put it on our kitchen fire.

Of course, Miss Playfair had to be told that Bernie had disappeared — since everyone else in the valley knew it by that time. She didn't seem very interested. After all, she'd never even met Bernie. He'd gone to live at Wally before she'd ever arrived at Deepwater so he wasn't important to her at all.

She was much more bothered about Ruth and never stopped asking Mother how she was and when she'd be coming back to school.

"I need her for the Pageant you see, Mrs Ross." she said more than once. "She's going to be Australia. It's a very important part. I'm afraid I'll just have to give it to someone else if Ruth doesn't come back to school soon. What exactly is the matter with her?"

Mother gave some vague answer and changed the subject.

I knew that Ruth must be eating less and less in the middle of the night. Her face had gone all thin and bony. Her eyes seemed sunken and hollow. She still wouldn't speak though I went down there three times a week to try to talk to her. To be honest, Ruth frightened me. She seemed to be miles away from us all in a silent world of her own. I thought she needed a doctor but Mrs Henschke just went on mixing drinks of herbs from the garden in cups of boiling water. Ruth refused to drink them. Her whole body was shrinking away inside her baggy cotton dress. I really began to fear that she might die. I began to think I'd have to find Bernie myself since no one else seemed to be able to find him. Bernie had to be told about Ruth. He had to know that she'd starve herself to death if he wouldn't come back home again.

I climbed up the hill to consult Mr Mallorie. He knew the country in our north east corner of the State better than anyone. He'd lived there the longest. And he'd known Bernie since the day he was born. Surely, I thought, he'd have some idea where a boy on the run might hide.

Mr Mallorie was digging a pit in his back yard. He worked slowly with long pauses between each shovelful of earth. He'd let go his trouser-legs to grasp the spade with both hands. I noticed that the trousers stayed up perfectly well with the old crossed braces that he always wore.

"Are you going to bury all your tins in it?" I asked, looking down into the gaping hole.

"Nope! I'm jist looking for water, lass. That spring of mine's still flowing quite well but it's the only one left at this end of the valley. Everyone's using it now. I could do with another spring. Jist to be on the safe side. So I'm digging for one."

"How do you know there's water under there?"

"I don't. I'm jist hoping. I've tried a couple of other spots but I didn't have no luck at all. I jist wish I had one of them magic twigs. Me father had the knack of it."

"What magic twigs?" I asked him.

"I suppose it's not really magic. More like a science, me Dad said. It's a way of finding water. You hold a forked twig between your two hands. And when you walk across water it points to the ground."

I laughed out loud.

"Have you ever tried it yourself, Mr Mallorie?"

"Not yet, lass. But I'm thinking of it. I got to get the right kind of twig. You can't do it with jist any old stick. It's got to be the right sort."

"What sort?"

"That's the trouble. I don't know. Me dad told me once but I've gone and forgotten it. So I jist stick to the digging."

He bent down over his spade again. The earth at the bottom of the hole seemed very dry to me.

"Mr Mallorie! I want to talk to you. We've got to find Bernie Henschke. Ruth'll die if he doesn't come back. She won't eat properly. Can't you think where he might've gone? Where would you go if you were fourteen and running away from people who called you horrible names?"

Mr Mallorie seemed glad to step up out of his hole. He squatted on his haunches and rubbed his veined hands together.

"Would you go to the city?" I demanded.

Mr Mallorie shook his head.

"Would you search for friends or relations?"

He shook his head again.

"Would you pretend you were older and try to join the army?"

"Never!" he said.

"Would you try to get a job?"

"No. That'd make it too easy for someone to find me. The

boss'd read the advertisements in the paper. He'd soon let on where I was. He'd want the reward. No, lass. I wouldn't never get a job."

"What *would* you do, then? You'd have to eat."

"I'd live rough. I'd make for the bush. Any boy with an ounce of common sense can live in the bush for months at a time. He can catch fish in the creeks. Or rabbits up on the ridges. Or even birds, if he's quick. He can make a kind of bark hut to sleep in at night. A mia-mia. I'd jist hang about in the bush till all the trouble had died down. No one wouldn't never set eyes on me."

"But you'd have no fire. Would you eat raw rabbits? I bet Bernie'd never do that. He'd be sick."

"I'd take a packet of lucifers with me before I ran. And a tinder-box."

Mr Mallorie's idea of living rough in the bush filled me with despair. There was so much wild bush in Victoria. Bernie could be anywhere. No one could possibly know where to start looking. But Mr Mallorie went on talking.

"I wouldn't never go too far from home, mind. The bush near home is always more friendly than the bush on the other side of the state. I'd feel safer if I knew I could walk in me own back door after a couple of hours' tramping. Not that I'd come back till I was good and ready. But I'd like to know I could – if I ever wanted to."

"So you mean Bernie could be hiding out in the bush only two hours' walk from here — only eight miles off?"

"Less than eight, I reckon. More like four or five."

"He couldn't be so near!" I said.

"Yep. He could, lass. Over the river there, on the wild side. Near some creek for water. Or further up into the foothills beyond our Track. Or in that rough country over the ridge behind us here."

This astonishing idea that Bernie could be quite close to home made me feel worse rather than better. Even if he was just over the river or up in the hills, how could we ever find him? The bush was thick. He was as lost as if he was stranded up in the Mallee somewhere.

"Why don't you signal?" asked Mr Mallorie.

"How?"

"Light a fire up here on the ridge at night. Hope he'd see it."

"But even if he did see it, how could he know we wanted him to come home? A fire is just a fire. It doesn't say anything."

"He'd be surprised to see it. He'd guess something was wrong."

I had my doubts about that.

"It's worth a try," Mr Mallorie went on. "I'll light one tonight. Plenty of dry wood up here for a fire. Too much in fact."

"What if it runs away from you? Gets out of control? Everything's tinder-dry in the valley. You could burn us all out."

Mr Mallorie laughed at me.

"I'm an old bushman, lass. Don't forget that. I know how to look after a fire. I've got me spring here for water. And I'd clear a wide break all around it before I started. Don't worry about that. I can handle a fire."

"But, Mr Mallorie, will you wait up till he comes? All night?"

He nodded.

"I suppose I might nod off now and then," he admitted. "But I'll stay by the fire. He'll see me right enough."

"I'd be scared to sit out all night," I admitted.

"No one's asking you to do it. I'm not scared. I'm used to the night. And I'll have me old stone with me. That keeps off the witches, you know. That's what me Dad always said." He chuckled to himself.

"I didn't mean witches," I said. I really thought he was a bit mad sometimes with all that peculiar talk of his stone and his magic twigs. I wasn't at all convinced by his plan. Lighting a fire for Bernie seemed such a long shot. But any plan was better than no plan.

"What'll I tell him, lass? If he does come?" asked Mr Mallorie, picking up his spade again.

"Tell him Ruth's very ill. All because of him. And tell him Hans has gone off to the war. They need him on the farm. Ask him to come home."

I found myself suddenly crying. Mr Mallorie stared at me in surprise. I wasn't ever one to cry, not even when I was a little kid and certainly not now I was fourteen. He fished in his pocket and pulled out a grubby handkerchief but I turned and fled down the hill. I felt too embarrassed at that unexpected rush of tears.

Once I was home again and working in the barn where no one could see me I was soon myself again. In fact I even began to feel an odd kind of happiness when I thought of Mr Mallorie's plan of lighting a fire. For the rest of that day I was full of hope and excitement. I looked out from our back verandah at night and saw the fire burning brightly, high on the ridge. I could imagine Mr Mallorie snoozing right beside it, his back against a tree. But when I raced up to see him early the next morning, straight after the milking, my hopes were dashed. Bernie hadn't come at all.

"I'll try it again, lass," said Mr Mallorie. "I'll light another fire tonight."

But I'd rather lost faith in his fires. I didn't believe Bernie could be so close after all. The blue hills kept their secrets to themselves.

The travelling photographer came to Deepwater that week. He always came along the valley once a year about that time to take a picture of all the children lined up outside the schools. Sometimes one of the families might want a photo of a new baby or an old grandma or even a prize bull. So the photographer generally did the rounds of the farms just in case. He came bumping along Gillespie's Track in a high covered wagon with all his equipment packed inside so he could develop and print his photographs in a few hours. He camped by the river for three or four days, the same as usual, and tethered his big grey horse to a tree. Everyone knew the photographer but none of us knew his name. He was a white-haired old chap with a bushy beard. He'd been on the roads taking photos in little settlements like ours for thirty years or more. He had a small fox-terrier — black and white — that ran behind his wagon when he was out on the Track and slept underneath it at night. That little dog was getting old but he was still full of life with his sharp ears pricked and his head cocked to one side. The dog and the man seemed to look more like each other every year.

Miss Playfair was excited when Dad told her the photographer had come. She didn't just want the usual formal photograph of the school children standing in straight rows outside the school. She wanted a special picture of her Pageant with all the kids dressed up as the countries of the Empire. The costumes were almost ready. She asked Dad if I could go in the photo — someone had to be Australia in place of Ruth and she suddenly thought of me. Dad wasn't too keen. We were busy. But he agreed when I pleaded with him. I still had my doubts about Miss Playfair herself, ever since the feather episode in the church, but I'd heard so much about that Pageant. She had talked of almost nothing else for weeks. Even the war had started to fade away into the background. So I was thrilled to be in it when Dad agreed. I was to be draped in the school's huge Australian flag that fluttered from the pole every Monday and I was to hold a bunch of late yellow wattle in my hand.

We all lined up on the front verandah of the school while the photographer erected his camera on its tripod. It was a splendid shining brown box made of wood with a black concertina-like bellows of leather joined on at the back. Fred Henschke was Canada and I stood right next to him. South Africa was there and New Zealand and India and Ceylon and lots of other countries. We knew them all already from the pink bits on the globe in the school. Ellie Craik was England in a long white nightdress with a paper crown on her head and a cardboard shield in her hand. Miss Playfair arranged us all carefully. I'd never seen her looking so beautiful. I even forgot about the feathers altogether for half an hour. She told us to smile as the photographer buried his snowy head under a black sheet. He adjusted the camera. His head came out again and he slid his first plate into position with a satisfying click.

"Watch the little birdie!" he cried and pressed the button at the end of a long black cord.

Some of those little kids really did think there was a bird inside his camera. I even used to think that myself once. I smiled hard and held on tighter to my wattle. I didn't feel entirely happy. It was all very well being Australia. I could see it was an important part. But Miss Playfair was much more interested in England. The photographer pulled out his first plate and pushed in the next. For this second photo, Ellie Craik stood on a box and we all clustered round her, looking up at her crown and smiling. I wished I could be England. It wasn't really fair. I was the oldest, after all. Ellie was only thirteen.

When the session was over, Miss Playfair took all the children back into school. I unwrapped my flag and went to watch the photographer climbing into the back of his covered cart.

"You can't come in I'm afraid, girlie," he said. "I've got to work in the pitch dark in here. Anyway there's only room for one."

I stepped back in disappointment.

"Here you are!" he said. "You can look through this pile of old photos if you like. I call them the rejects. They're the ones that didn't come out too well. And the ones that no one ever claimed. There must be fifty or more. I ought to throw them away I suppose. Some of them go back years and years. Here you are, girlie."

I took the bundle of reject photographs to the school verandah and looked through them half-heartedly at first, flicking quickly on from one to the next. I knew I couldn't spend long. Dad would be waiting for me. But it was fascinating to see the sepia-coloured schools that all looked much the same with their rows of children and their stiff lady-teachers. No one as beautiful as our Miss Playfair, I thought to myself with satisfaction. And in amongst the schools were fat babies in long frilly christening robes, all fuzzy at the edges. And a wedding couple or two.

Then I gasped! I stared at the last photo in the pile. It was Bernie! Not last year's photo or the year before that. It was this year! I knew that shirt he had on, even though it was all crushed and dirty. I raced across the school yard to the wagon and banged on the door.

"What's up?" came the muffled and angry voice of the photographer from inside. "Don't you open that door! You'll ruin everything if you do!"

"It's this photo of Bernie!" I shouted back. My voice sounded strange, even to my ears. "Bernie Henschke! He's lost! We're all looking for him! Where did you take it? Where is he?"

"Wait a minute, girlie! Wait a minute! I don't know what you're talking about. When I've finished this developing, I'll come out and have a look."

I could hardly wait. I danced around the cart, wildly waving the picture of Bernie. I showed it to the horse, holding it right up close to his blinkered eyes. I bent down under the cart and showed it to the dog. I even kissed it — though I made sure first that no one was looking at me out of the school windows. No one was. Miss Playfair didn't allow that sort of thing. I was quite safe. But I felt pretty silly when I realized what I'd done.

It seemed an age before the photographer opened up the door in his wagon.

"Now, what's all this?" he asked, smiling down at me from the top step.

"It's this photo! This boy! Bernie Henschke! We don't know where he is. He's been missing for weeks. And his sister's sick and his Dad needs him on the farm! Where did you see him?"

The photographer took the photograph from me and stared at it, frowning. He didn't speak.

"Oh, can't you remember? Please!" I begged him.

"I remember him all right, girlie. I'm just trying to think of the name of the place. Not so far from here, it was, and only a week or two back. Nice lad. Fair hair. Needed a comb and a cut. But he was well-mannered, I'll say that. He asked me for a job. I didn't have a job to give him. There's only work for one in this van. But we had a long chat about this and that. Water mainly. Water and the drought."

"But why did you take his picture?"

"I don't know, girlie. Just liked his face, I suppose. He helped me pack up the van one night outside one of those little schools. And he brushed down the horse for me. He knew how to handle a horse all right. And then I took his photo. He didn't seem to mind."

"What school? Which school? Where was it?" I demanded.

The photographer scratched his white head.

"I'm damned if I know," he said. "Only a week or two back, like I said. These little places are all much the same, you know. I can't remember one from another."

"But don't you write them down somewhere? In a book? In case someone wants to order an extra photo?"

"Yes," he said. "I do. With the dates too. Maybe that'll help."

He dived back into his van and came out holding a blue exercise book with the multiplication tables printed on the back. He opened it up. There was a list in his big careful writing of the little settlements up Gillespie's Track from Wallaceville. Talisker, Longstone Bend, Burnett's Bridge.

"What's this place again?" he asked, looking up at the school. "Kanyul?"

"Deepwater. The school used to be at Kanyul. It was shifted."

He nodded and wrote the name 'Deepwater' slowly in pencil at the end of his list.

"It wasn't any of these places," he said. "Let's go back to last week."

He turned back a page in the book. Another list. All the schools in the next valley, over the ridge. Bailey's Bank, Kirkwood, Sheltie, McGowan's Plain, Stonyknowe.

He shook his head and turned back another page. Another valley.

Grahamslaw, Yellow Gully, Syme's Spring, Last Creek.

"I dunno!" he said. "It must have been one of these places. I left old Syme's place two weeks ago and pushed on to Last

Creek. Dreary place it is, too. That was about the time I saw the lad, I reckon. But I can't be sure. And anyway, he wasn't stopping there. He was moving on. He told me that. Moving on."

"But where?" I cried. I was angry that he couldn't remember more.

"He didn't say, girlie," said the photographer.

I'd never heard of any of those places in his list. I borrowed his pencil and wrote them down quickly on the back of Bernie's photo. Grahamslaw, Yellow Gully, Syme's Spring, Last Creek.

"Can I keep it? The photograph? It might help us find him. The only one Mr Henschke had to give the police is three years old and all smudgy. This one's clear."

The photographer looked pleased.

"I do take a good picture," he said, "though I say it myself. Yes, you can keep it, girlie. You're welcome. And if I see the lad again, I'll tell him he's wanted at home. Urgent, will I say?"

"Yes! Yes! Urgent!" I said and ran off with the photograph straight down the Track to the Henschkes' farm.

7. The Day of the North Wind

Mr Henschke rode the whole way into Wallaceville that same day. He took the photograph in his pocket. But the police had completely lost interest in looking for Bernie. He told Dad about it hours later after the milking was finished.

"There's a war on!" the sergeant had said rudely to Mr Henschke, handing the photograph back to him. "We can't waste our time looking for lost kids. You Germans ought to take more care of your families. They're your responsibility, after all."

"I'm not a German, mate," Mr Henschke had said to him. "I'm an Australian. Just like you." And he'd walked out of the police station and ridden the twenty miles home again.

That last hopeless visit to talk to the police was a turning point for the Henschkes. It was then that they began to withdraw. They even stopped going to church on Sundays. They kept all the children home from school. Mrs Henschke taught them herself on their back verandah. They didn't go to the local store any more since the Pollocks had refused outright to sell them any sugar. Mr Henschke drove his cart into Wally and loaded it up with enough flour and sugar to last for six months or more. He bought boxes of candles and tins of kerosene for the lamps and feed for the chooks. Everything else they produced for themselves on the farm — meat, eggs, fruit, vegetables. They made their own soap. The firewood came from their land.

The Henschkes were almost self-sufficient. All they needed was a couple of buckets of water every day from Mr Mallorie's spring. He was glad to give it. He never turned against the Henschkes. They went up the hill for their water early in the morning before anyone else was about. Apart from Mr Mallorie — and they hardly ever saw him — our family was the only link the Henschkes had with the outside world. All the other families in the valley seemed somehow to have forgotten them — or to be afraid of them. Afraid of old neighbours they'd known for years! It was incredible. Dad offered to handle Mr Henschke's buying of seed and the selling of his oat crop and his wool and his butter. Not that there was much to sell. Everyone's yield was down to half or less. Everyone was losing stock from the drought and the Henschkes were no exception. They were burning and burying their dead animals just like everyone else.

Mother asked for their letters at the store — there were almost never any at all — and she walked down to see Mrs Henschke once a week. They talked over a cup of tea but I was never there so I don't know what they talked about. The war, I suppose, and the boys. Mother made me keep going too though I didn't want to. She said I had to talk to Ruth. But that was hopeless. Ruth's family might have withdrawn from the valley but Ruth was withdrawing from life itself. Those herb teas weren't going to save her. I knew that. Whenever I went down there they never talked about anything but Ruth. They stood round the bed and discussed her just as if she wasn't lying there listening to them all. I began to hate every visit I made to that place and most of all I hated sitting by Ruth's bed, trying to persuade her to talk or to eat. It made me feel sick in the stomach. She looked like a skeleton. Like a ghost. She wasn't the person I used to know at all. But her thick fair hair was brushed as thoroughly and plaited as neatly as ever. Mrs Henschke did it every day. I think it made her feel she was in control of the situation — but she wasn't at all. And neither was I.

I was astonished at the way the Schoolie reacted to all this. When Ruth had stopped coming to school, weeks earlier, Miss Playfair had pestered us with questions. But now that all the Henschke children stayed at home, she asked us nothing at all. She simply distributed their parts in the Pageant to other children in the school without a word of explanation. Most of them had to be two countries at once though none of them minded that. They were pleased. Miss Playfair never mentioned the Henschkes again. She didn't even bother to collect the scarves they'd finally finished knitting for the soldiers. I used to see them, neatly folded in a pile on Mrs Henschke's sewing machine. For Miss Playfair, it was simply as if the Henschke family had ceased to exist. Dad and Mother and I sensed that we'd better keep quiet about the Henschkes when Miss Playfair was with us at tea time or in the kitchen every evening. At those times we didn't mention them any more than she did. Only when she was safely away at the school and we three were alone did we dare to speak about them. Even then we lowered our voices. And at church too, when we were with all the other families from our end of the valley, we avoided the whole subject altogether. No one else even used their name any more. They were just called 'the Germans' or even 'the Huns'. Dad and Mother came in for some cold looks when it was known that we kept in touch with the Henschkes. That was seen as shocking disloyalty to king and country. So we kept completely silent about our visits. Mother gave up asking for their letters at the post office in the Pollocks' store. It didn't seem worthwhile.

That strange shift of feeling about the Henschkes, in a matter of a few months, from open and easy friendship with neighbours everyone had known for a lifetime or more to suspicion and even hatred towards some fearful enemy has always puzzled me. The Henschkes had not changed. They were the same people. But now they were seen as 'Huns' and as a terrible danger to the whole community — indeed to the whole nation. It was ridiculous. And yet, although we kept up our secret links with the Henschkes, we were not brave enough to challenge the suspicion or to persuade anyone else to take up their friendship with 'the German family' again. We were almost as bad as the rest. That's what puzzles me. How on earth did we let it happen?

Only Mr Mallorie was different. Every time he saw us, he asked about Bernie, whether Miss Playfair was in the room or not.

"No news at all!" we muttered quickly and changed the subject. We didn't quite look him in the eye as we spoke. But Mr Mallorie wasn't to be put off so easily. He still asked again the next time he dropped in. As he didn't ever go to church and seldom saw any neighbours, I'm not sure if he even knew that the position of the Henschkes had changed.

"I'm still lighting that fire for the lad," he said to me on one of his visits. "Once a week. Every Sat'dee night. May do no good but it can't do no harm."

I always looked out to see the fire as darkness fell on Saturday nights but I had no hope that it would ever bring Bernie home again. I felt he'd gone for good.

Meanwhile, the war was getting under way. Back in October, Laurie had written to say goodbye. He was off with hundreds of other lads to Western Australia. That was the gathering point. He sounded so excited and happy. Early in November he sailed from Fremantle to the training camp in Egypt. We had a couple of letters from there eventually but not till well after Christmas. The heat and the flies and the dirty streets — that's all he ever wrote about. And the pyramids. He actually saw them! Col Douglas was with him over there but the other boys from our end of the valley, Martin and Hans (under their new names) and Bill Craik and Ronnie Douglas had sailed on a different ship and he had no idea where they were. In fact they weren't far from him in another camp in Egypt. The Douglases had a letter from Ronnie and we were able to work out where they all were. The Henschke boys didn't ever write home. That wasn't like them. Perhaps the letters got lost somewhere in the post. But Mrs Henschke never complained. She just borrowed Laurie's two letters from Mother and read them out to her family. That seemed to satisfy them.

"It's a grand life for those youngsters!" Mr Douglas said to Dad one Sunday outside the church, grinning with delight. "Wish we'd had that chance ourselves, eh Alec? They'll learn a thing or two over there, I reckon. See the world."

Dad nodded and laughed.

"How are you getting on without the boys now, Frank?" he

asked. "Will you look for someone to help you out?"

"No. I've gone one better than that. I've bought a milking machine. It just came last week. Does the job in half the time."

Dad was stunned.

"A milking machine! But they run on electricity, don't they? There's no electricity in this valley! You know that, Frank."

"Bought me own little vacuum pump," said Mr Douglas proudly. "She's a beauty too. Pounds away there just outside the cow shed. She drives the motor and the motor drives the milking machine. You must come and have a look at her, Alec. We can use the motor at night to drive a little generator too. Might even light up the house one of these days. That's what the wife'd like."

That certainly gave us something to talk about over Sunday dinner. A milking machine! And they might even light up the house with electric lights! Dad was sceptical. Cows needed human hands on their teats, he said. But Mother was rather envious.

"Electric light!" she kept murmuring to herself as she cleared away the dishes.

Mr Craik didn't buy a milking machine. He really did sell up — just as he'd threatened to do. The drought had hit him harder than anyone. His sheep and cows were pathetic skinny creatures. He sold the lot in the first week of December. Dad bought some of them himself and led them up the Track to our place. Most of the other farmers at our end bought the rest of the stock between them. No one really wanted more animals but everyone felt sorry for the Craiks and the price was dirt cheap.

There was no farewell party when the Craiks left. One day they were there at their farm as usual and the next morning we heard at the store that they'd gone in the night, with all their possessions piled up onto two carts. Mr Craik didn't get much for his land. You never do in the middle of a drought. And the man who bought it didn't come near the valley for years. He just waited for better times. So the Craiks' house stood empty with all the doors and windows shut tight against the dust and all the blinds pulled down. Their garden shrivelled up completely that summer with no one to water the plants with the used washing water. At harvest time no one bothered to bring in their scraggy oats or their wheat. The crops just dried brown in the paddocks and blew away in the wind.

So before Christmas came in 1914, the war and the drought had changed the lives of those two families. For the Douglases with their brand new milking machine, it was a time of experiment and hope, in spite of the drought. They took a risk and eventually it paid off. They're still the richest family in the valley today. But for the Craiks it was the end of the road. I don't know where they went, with their three girls and the two little boys perched up on top of the carts. We never heard of them again. After the war the news went round that one of the Craik boys had been killed in France. We never knew if it was Gordon or Bill.

Miss Playfair was terribly upset when she heard the Craiks had gone. She had to double up still more parts in her Pageant only a week before the great performance. With the loss of five Henschkes and now four Craiks, her school had suddenly fallen from twenty-six children to only seventeen. That was including the five kids from Kanyul. I think she began to worry that her school might fade away altogether. She had fixed the date of the Pageant for December 10th. She said I could be England since Ellie Craik had gone but I couldn't be Australia as well because England was so important. I had to give up the Australian flag to Mollie Logan who was India as well. I thought she'd look pretty silly with a pink sari wrapped around her and the Australian flag draped over her head but Miss Playfair seemed pleased with the effect. I would've liked to wear that sari. Miss Playfair's father had bought it in the city and sent it up specially. Mrs Pollock at the store told Mother that Miss Playfair got far more letters and parcels than anyone else at Deepwater. We even heard that she'd had a letter from Col Douglas on his way to Egypt but I didn't know if that was true. She'd never met him, after all, but I wondered if perhaps his family had written and told him all about her and about what she was doing to help win the war. He might have felt grateful. Or perhaps, I thought, she even wrote to him first — just out of the blue. It's not very lady-like to write first. I know that. But in war-time good manners can change. She might've wanted to tell him how much she admired his courage. I began to think that was the most likely way it could've all started. Anyway, if she did get a letter from Col Douglas, we never saw it and she didn't read it out to the kids in school.

Miss Playfair's craze for making flags and sticking cuttings into her War Book had waned a bit by the beginning of December. Her mind was full of the Pageant and anyway the war news coming through from her father wasn't good. The great British victories didn't seem to be happening quite as he'd predicted. In fact they weren't happening at all. The Germans were winning. I felt strangely relieved. I was sorry, of course, that we weren't winning the war yet, but I was glad not to have to spend my evenings making flags. I'd found it so exciting at first. Not the flags themselves but helping Miss Playfair. Gradually that excitement had faded and my feelings about Miss Playfair had become more complicated. In some curious way, I almost blamed her for Bernie's disappearance and Ruth's refusal to eat though really she had nothing to do with either. I certainly did blame her for sending Bill Craik and Ronnie Douglas and Hans Henschke off to the war with her white feathers. But no one else knew that she had done that. I never told a soul — not even Mother. Sometimes I didn't quite believe it myself. She still fascinated me with her walk and her talk. My eyes kept coming back to her in spite of myself. But I couldn't admire her so utterly as I'd done in her first weeks in our house. I found I was quite glad that she often went to her room after tea and didn't come out again. I used to sit on in the kitchen with Mother and Dad for an hour, knitting a few more slow rows of the soldier's scarf till I went off to bed, exhausted with another day's work on the parching farm.

The day of the Pageant came at last. Dad had agreed to release me from the farm straight after the early milking —

though not without a lot of grumbling. The Pageant wasn't starting till two o'clock in the afternoon but Miss Playfair wanted to spend the whole morning going through the final dress rehearsal. I hadn't been to any of the other practices. They'd all been in school time and Dad wouldn't let me go. Miss Playfair had just had to take my part for me but now, on the great day itself, I learnt where I was to stand, when I was to move and what I was supposed to do. Pageants are very much easier than plays, I will say that. You don't have any lines to learn — or we didn't in that Pageant anyway. Miss Playfair had written the script herself — all in a kind of poetry — and she read it out in a loud clear voice while we moved about the stage. The 'stage' was just the school verandah. All the long benches and the chairs had been carried out and arranged in rows in the playground for the audience to sit on. They were only a few feet from the verandah where we were going to perform so everyone would be able to see and hear well.

A hot north wind had sprung up early that morning and was tearing at the dry leaves of the gum trees around the school fence. A north wind always makes children restless and bad-tempered. It had that effect on Miss Playfair too so the morning's rehearsal was an unhappy business. None of us seemed to be able to do exactly what she wanted. The costumes kept slipping off our shoulders at the wrong moment and blowing about in the wind. The strange dramatic voice Miss Playfair used for reading out her poem made the little kids giggle. It was so different from her usual voice. Nothing went right. By lunch time Miss Playfair was exasperated.

"You'd better all just take off those costumes," she said tersely. "You can put on your ordinary clothes and go down to the shelter-shed to eat your sandwiches. I'll call you when it's time to get ready. And do try to do better this afternoon. Everyone will be watching you. Don't forget that."

She went back inside the school to eat her own lunch at her desk. I looked through the window. She had her head in her hands.

I joined all the little kids down in the shelter-shed.

"Look," I said. "Poor Miss Playfair's nearly crying in there."

Someone laughed. I soon stopped that.

"No. It's not funny," I said. "We've got to try to do the thing properly this afternoon. We can't let her down in front of all the parents. Come on! Let's go through those movements again till we get them right!"

Steve Morison groaned.

"Oh Char Ross! You're too bossy! You're as bad as that Miss Playfair! Just because she lives in your house, you think you're someone!"

"Shut up, Steve!" said Phyllis Douglas. "Char's right. Let's try it just once more. We'll give that Schoolie a nice surprise. She thinks we're all stupid — but we're not really."

Slowly the kids put their thick sandwiches back inside their newspaper wrappings and laid them down carefully on the bench along the back of the shed. They stood up. I took charge.

"Right!" I said. "First of all, I come onto the stage like this and I stand in the centre. Then, as Miss Playfair reads all the bits out of her poem, I beckon you in one by one. Mollie, you come first. Run in now and kneel down here. That's right, Mollie. Now Sylvia. You're next. Good. Come on now Steve. Phyllis. Jeff. Sid. Now you five Kanyul kids can all come on together. That's it. Don't push each other. Now Jack. Ken. Norm. Grace. John. Annie."

One by one they ran towards me from the far side of the shelter-shed. They knelt down on the hard dirt floor and gazed up at me. They were all grinning. They weren't really supposed to grin. The Pageant was meant to be serious.

"Now when Miss Playfair starts talking about the enemy, we all look one way — over there to the left — and we hold hands. We're supposed to look fierce. To scare off the enemy."

They all frowned and looked terribly fierce. I found it hard not to laugh.

"That's good," I said. "Now we shake our fists at the enemy."

They all shook their fists.

"We should be looking the other way!" muttered Sid Pollock.

"No we shouldn't! Miss Playfair said to look to the left!" said Mollie Logan.

"But the Huns live the other way! That Henschke family. 'The Bosch', my Dad calls them — and he's right too!"

"Yeah! We should look that way!" said his sister Annie. "Henschke Hunschke!"

Some of the children began to turn to the right.

"Don't be silly!" I shouted angrily. "The Henschkes aren't Huns at all. Now look to the left! The way Miss Playfair said."

They all swung their heads obediently back to the left. The hot wind whipped the dust from the playground into our eyes.

"Now when she gets to the last part, I have to lead the way and we march all around the verandah. Mr Logan'll be playing his bagpipes. And we sing. We're supposed to be winning the war. So we've all got to smile and wave our flags or our wattle or our maple leaves or whatever we've got in our hands. Right! Off we go!"

I glided triumphantly around the shelter-shed, holding myself as tall as I could. The kids trailed after me in a ragged bunch. I stopped and arranged them neatly in pairs and we tried again. I led them off as we sang our farewell song — the only time we actually had to open our mouths in the entire performance.

"Rule Britannia! Britannia rule the waves!
Britons never never never shall be slaves!"

"Can't we eat our sandwiches now, Char?" moaned Sylvia.

"Yes," I said. "Eat up. That Pageant's much better now. But don't fidget when she's reading out the poem. Keep still and look at me!"

I sat down beside them on the bench and ate my own sandwiches. It was funny the way the little boys respected me a bit now that I worked on the farm with Dad. They'd never bothered with me at all when I was still at school but now they clustered round me in the shelter-shed and asked me, man to man, what feed we were using now for the stock and how long

I thought the river would hold out and how many ewes we'd lost in November. I didn't have any cheerful news to give them. Our farm was in the same bad state as theirs. But I don't think that in all the years since then I've ever felt as important as I did that day — the day I was a real farmer among the boys at the school and played the part of England in Miss Playfair's Pageant of the British Empire.

"Time to get ready, children!" Miss Playfair called down to us from the school window. She seemed to have recovered. She looked all calm and beautiful again.

The parents started arriving just before two o'clock. The Kanyul families came first in their buggies. The Deepwater people just walked along from the farms or rode their horses and tied them to the fence. The mothers had on their long summer dresses and the men were in shirt sleeves and black waistcoats. They never liked to take off those waistcoats of theirs even on the hottest days and that day was certainly hot. It was the kind of day Dad used to call a 'stinker'. The north wind had frayed everyone's nerves and none of the parents looked very enthusiastic about coming to see the Pageant. But they sat down willingly enough on the seats in the playground. Mother and Dad were there, of course, and the Logans, the Morisons, the Douglases, the three Kanyul families and the Pollocks from the store. Young Donny Pollock had stayed behind to mind the shop. They weren't allowed to leave the Post Office unattended. But I don't think he would have had any customers that afternoon. Even Mr Mallorie came shuffling down from his ridge at the last minute and sat next to Dad in the front row.

I was inside the school with all the children. We were putting the finishing touches to our costumes and looking out of the window as the audience filled up the seats. Miss Playfair was excited and happy. I kept thinking back to the day in September when those same families had all been there for the shifting of the school. It had been only three months earlier. The Craiks had been there then and the Henschkes. Everyone had been working and laughing together. Deepwater seemed strange now. The place wasn't the same at all.

It was time to begin. Miss Playfair walked out onto the verandah and welcomed the parents. She explained that most of the children had to represent more than one country. I thought she looked very nice in her grey cotton skirt and a white tucked blouse with its high neck and her gold locket. She nodded to Mr Logan who stood up in front of the audience, tucked his bagpipes under his arm, and blew his first long droning note. Then he played a bright military march. That set everyone's feet tapping and every face smiling. We all loved the pipes in the valley. The north wind didn't seem so bad. When he'd finished, Miss Playfair unrolled her script and began to read in that special high voice with all the words very clearly pronounced.

> *"Mother England in her Hour of Need!*
> *A Pageant of the British Empire*
> *by the children of the Deepwater School."*

The audience clapped politely.

"Hurry up, Char!" whispered Mollie right behind me, giving me a push. "It's time for you to go on!"

I stepped out of the school door and onto the verandah. The rough boards pricked my bare feet. The wind tugged at my silky white nightdress. Miss Playfair herself had lent it to me. It was beautiful. I had a band of elastic round the middle to hitch it up so it wouldn't trail on the floor. I held on to my crown so the wind couldn't blow it off and I grasped my cardboard shield with the other hand. I'd painted a good bold Union Jack on the shield. I was quite an expert now after all those evenings with the little flags at the kitchen table.

I stood completely still in the centre of the stage while Miss Playfair declaimed her opening lines. I did think it was so clever the way she'd made the whole thing rhyme.

> *Mother England, Queen of nations,*
> *Ruler over land and sea,*
> *Hear the voices of thy children*
> *As they sing their praise to thee.*

> *Call them from the steamy jungle*
> *Call them from the desert wild,*
> *Call them from the far-flung islands,*
> *Call each meek and loving child.*

That was the moment when I had to turn towards the school door to beckon in the countries of the Empire, one by one. I hoped they'd manage to come in in the right order. It would be awful if Ceylon came in when Miss Playfair was talking about Rhodesia. There was Mollie dressed as India and Australia, holding the flag tightly round her shoulders and running towards me in her pink sari. We were off to a good start.

> *India, jewel of Britain's Empire,*
> *Enters first to take her stand,*
> *With her comes our dear Australia,*
> *Rich and fertile, blesséd land.*

I never liked that line much. Didn't Miss Playfair know about the drought? The country wasn't rich and fertile at all and it wasn't blesséd either. 'Curséd', Dad used to call it. Still, I suppose in a poem you can't really mention the dried up rivers or the dying sheep. It wouldn't be very nice.

"Well done, Mollie!" shouted Mr Logan and clapped his hands loudly together.

"Shhh!" said Mrs Logan, looking embarrassed.

I beckoned to Sylvia Morison in her tartan skirt, her cheerful face blackened all over with boot polish.

> *Bonnie Scotland, thick with heather,*
> *Where grey lochs and mountains meet,*
> *Bring the Gold Coast, rich with treasure,*
> *Lay it all at England's feet.*

Sylvia stumbled a bit but recovered her balance and knelt down to place her box of gold nuggets on the floor beside me.

Steve came in next as South Africa and Rhodesia; then Phyllis with red paper maple leaves stitched onto her dress and an empty rum bottle in her hand. She was Canada and

Jamaica. Mr Mallorie had supplied the bottle. Jeff got a good clap from the audience as New Zealand. Sid was supposed to be Ireland and the Bahamas but Ireland definitely had the better of it. The five little Kanyul kids came next — they were British Guiana, Bermuda, British Honduras, Bechuanaland and a place I'd never even heard of called Labuan. Little Jack Morison was Gibraltar. Then came Ceylon and Malta, the Malay States, Nigeria and Sierra Leone, Trinidad and British East Africa. Last of all came Annie Pollock as Aden.

I can't remember the whole poem now after all this time but I do know that Miss Playfair had managed to say something really kind about every single country. One bit I can still recall was the verse for Jack Morison and Kenny Douglas.

> Solid Rock, O strong Gibraltar,
> Bastion of our Empire free!
> Now two islands, one is Malta,
> One Ceylon, where men grow tea.

Kenny was carrying his mother's best china tea-pot. She was very good to lend it, I thought. I could see her looking rather anxious as he came running in with it. He put it down carefully beside me. Mrs Douglas smiled with relief. Her tea-pot was safe. Now Miss Playfair lowered her voice dramatically and spoke of the Enemy. The kids stood up and we all turned at once to the left and looked fierce. We shook our fists.

> Rally round your Mother Country!
> Stand together, side by side!
> Face the foe! He will not conquer!
> Fight till death to break his pride!

"Hear! Hear!" called Mr Douglas and everyone clapped.

Now it was the moment for me to lead all the countries of the Empire in the march of triumph. I loved that part. Mr Logan stood up again and gave a skirl on his pipes. We burst into Rule Britannia and round and round we went. Finally we made our exit in through the open door to the school. Mr Logan went on playing till the last one of us had left the stage.

"You were wonderful, Char!" said one of the little Kanyul

kids, looking up at me in admiration and stroking the silk of my nightdress. Yes, that was a happy moment. We trooped out to the verandah again to take our bow. The mothers and fathers were all smiling and clapping. Miss Playfair followed us back into the school. She was flushed with delight at our performance.

"I really had no idea you could do it so well!" she said to us in astonishment. "You were wonderful!"

"Char helped us!" burst out Jack Morison. "She made us practise in the shelter-shed at lunch time!"

Miss Playfair turned and smiled at me. That was a good moment too.

I don't know why the thought of Ruth and Bernie had to come into my mind at that very minute but it did. They weren't there. None of the Henschkes were there. And all the Craiks had gone. And we hadn't had the puppets at the school that year. They were hidden away somewhere in the dark with the German Bible. My sense of happiness drained suddenly away. Something was badly wrong.

8. The Wild Cherry Tree

Miss Playfair had only another week with us before the Christmas holidays were to begin. Then Dad would drive her into Wally in the buggy with her case and she'd be off to the city to stay at home with her father till early in February and the new school year. Schoolies all over the State used to long for the end of that term before Christmas. Perhaps they still do. The sun always shone fiercer and hotter through November and December; the children in the iron-roofed schools became tireder and more difficult; Christmas itself was looming with all its excitement. The very minute the last school day was over, the teachers rushed to their trains from all the back-blocks and converged on the city. Miss Playfair would be one of hundreds of them when she stepped out onto Spencer Street Station in Melbourne at the end of the school year.

Two nights before she was to go, Mr Mallorie dropped in to see us. Miss Playfair was quite used to his sudden appearances now and was no more surprised to see him coming in the kitchen door than we were. He sat down beside Dad. Mother dished him up a good helping of shepherd's pie.

"Not a bad Pageant you put on the other day there, Miss," he said when his first sharp hunger had been satisfied. "I liked that bit with the tea-pot. Young Kenny Douglas. I couldn't help laughing. You done a real good job."

"Thank you," said Miss Playfair, flushing with pleasure. She knew Mr Mallorie wasn't one to fling praise idly around. "I'm so glad you enjoyed it. I do hope the children will remember the message."

"The message?" Mr Mallorie looked puzzled.

"I mean the whole idea behind my Pageant," she said earnestly, leaning forward. "About how England really needs each one of us in her struggle against the Kaiser. Winning a war isn't easy, you know, Mr Mallorie. It means sacrifice!"

He nodded.

"Too right," he said. "War always does."

"More shepherd's pie, Mr Mallorie?" said Mother. She looked worried. I knew she was hoping that Laurie wouldn't have to be the sacrifice.

"Don't mind if I do," he said and passed his plate.

When we'd all finished eating and Mother had made a cup of tea to end the meal, Mr Mallorie pushed back his chair.

"I was wondering, Miss," he said, turning to Miss Playfair, one hand diving into his trouser pocket, "if you'd like to take that stone of mine down to the city to show your Dad. Jist for a lend, mind! Not to keep. I'm not dead yet. You can have it when I'm gone. Unless I change me mind about that. But he jist might like to see it. Seeing as it was his old Dad that gave it to me, sixty years ago or more."

He took the stone out of his pocket and held it towards her.

"Oh yes," she said politely but without much enthusiasm, I thought. "I'm sure my father will be most interested. I'll take good care of it, Mr Mallorie. You can be sure of that. And I'll bring it back to you in the New Year."

"I was just thinking," Mr Mallorie went on, "that your Dad might be able to find out somethink about me stone. What river it comes from — if it comes from a river. I'd like to know. I reckon they know that kind of thing down in the city."

Miss Playfair looked uncertain. She turned the stone round in her hand. "Yes," she murmured. "Perhaps he could ask at the museum. Somewhere like that. If he has the time."

I had the distinct impression that she didn't really want to be lumbered with that stone. Her suitcase was heavy enough already. I remembered the weight of it.

"And I've finished off another scarf for you, Miss," said Mr Mallorie. "For the soldiers, I mean. I'll bring it down to the school tomorrer. You'll be sending them off soon, I suppose."

"I'm taking them down to Melbourne myself," she said.

"It's safer that way. How's yours coming on, Charlotte?"

"Nearly finished," I said. That wasn't quite true but I couldn't bear to disappoint her.

"I thought I might tackle one of them balaclavas next," said Mr Mallorie. "They go right over yer head, you know. Keep out the cold. I'm finding the scarves a bit too boring. Jist two plain, two purl, on and on."

Miss Playfair frowned.

"Balaclavas are very difficult," she said, "and I'm afraid I haven't a pattern."

"Don't bother about a pattern, Miss. I can work it out all right in me head. I've done socks without no pattern so I'll manage a balaclava all right. Can you give me the wool?"

She nodded.

"Yes. There's plenty of wool. A new bundle came just last week."

"I'll pick it up tomorrer, then," he said, "when I bring the scarf down the hill. I thought I might jist look through me Dad's old papers tonight. I've got a shoe-box full of them up there in the hut. Mostly jist rubbish — but there jist might be somethink of your Grandpa's among them. A photo or a letter or somethink of the kind. Seeing as they were such good friends. I haven't opened that box for years."

"It's very kind of you, Mr Mallorie," said Miss Playfair. She was still polite — she always was — but a bit more chilly. I could see that she didn't really want anything much to do with this toothless old man. She didn't relish the thought that he'd known her grandfather at all. Even his perfectly knitted scarves for the soldiers didn't alter her distaste for him.

"Your father probably threw away all that kind of thing before he died, Mr Mallorie," said Mother. "People don't seem to keep old letters, do they?"

"I'll jist have a look," said Mr Mallorie. "Well, I'll be off up the hill. It's a fine clear night for the stars out there, Alec."

"I'll walk some of the way with you," said Dad.

Dad always loved the stars. He often had a walk around the paddocks on his own at night, just to look at them, and he never missed a chance of climbing up towards the ridge with

Mr Mallorie. He liked the stars best when there was no moon at all. Once your eyes had got used to the dark, he used to say, you could find your way by the light of the stars. He often said that if you were lost in the bush you could get yourself safely home again if you followed the stars. Of course you had to know them. That's why he'd taught me the names of all the constellations and where in the sky to look for them, winter and summer. I still think of him even now, when I look up at the stars.

Two days later and Miss Playfair had gone. The house seemed strangely empty without her. The door of her room, normally shut, stood open to the verandah. Mother gave the whole room what she called a 'good going over'. I found her shaking her mop and her duster out in the back yard when the job was done.

"I will say this," she said to me. "That Miss Playfair always keeps her room nice and tidy. She's an example to you, Char. That's how a real lady looks after her things. You can see she's had a good upbringing, even though her poor mother's dead. When I went into the room this morning, there wasn't one thing out of place. Not even a scrap of paper on the floor or an empty cotton-reel under the bed. Not even a thread on the mat or the chair an inch crooked. You'd never even know someone had been living in there since September. It's as neat as a new pin."

I sighed. I didn't think I could ever keep a room like that. I wasn't even sure that I wanted to. But I did want to be a lady like Miss Playfair so I said I'd try. I knew I'd love to hear Mother say that my room was as 'neat as a new pin'.

"Did Mr Mallorie find any photos or old letters for Miss Playfair?" I asked her. "To take down to her father?"

Mother shook her head.

"No photos. No letters. Nothing much of interest at all. His father's will was there, I think, and his marriage certificate. Mr Mallorie says he didn't even know he had that certificate. It's very old. The date on it's 1847, I think. He didn't want to part with it, of course, so he's copied it all out for Miss Playfair."

"But why on earth would she want that?"

"Well it seems her grandfather was the witness to the marriage. Or one of them, anyway. Mr Mallorie showed me the certificate this morning. I didn't read it all but I noticed the date and I saw that signature clearly enough — Robert Somerville Playfair. He had a good bold hand, that grandfather of hers. It won't look nearly so fine, copied out in Mr Mallorie's writing," she laughed.

"Can he write?" I asked in surprise.

"Char! Of course he can write. Writing goes with reading. He's a great reader, Mr Mallorie is. He's got quite a little store of books up there in his hut and he reads them over and over. No spectacles either. He used to read aloud to his mother. And sing her the old songs."

"What old songs?"

"The ones she used to sing to him when he was a little boy, he told me. Old Scottish songs. 'Ye banks and braes o' bonnie Doon'. 'Loch Lomond'. That kind of song. When she was very old, she'd ask him to sing to her and he'd sing all those old favourites, one by one. He often used to come down the hill and ask me about the words. He knew all the first verses but he couldn't always remember the rest. I knew them so I helped him out. She was fond of hymns too and the metrical psalms. She loved those psalms best of all. He used to sing them all to her. 'I to the hills' and 'Now Israel may say' and 'I joyed when to'. All those ones. He was a good son to his mother. I'll never forget how well he took care of her in those last years of her life."

"When was all that, Mother?" I asked.

"About twenty years ago. Or a bit more. Before you and Laurie were born. I was just a young bride in those days."

She smiled to herself, remembering.

I giggled at the thought of Mother as a young bride.

"Don't you laugh, my girl," she said, "or you'll never be a bride yourself! All this farm work! It's not right!"

"I don't care!" I said, suddenly angry with her, "Who wants to be a bride? I like the farm!"

"Let's hope this war's soon over," she said, "and Laurie

safely home again. Then we can all get back to normal."

Dad came into the back yard.

"Two more ewes on their last legs, Char. Come on. I need another pair of hands."

I ran to help him. Mother sighed.

I was so used to the sight of those thin, staggering animals now that I no longer felt any sense of shock or surprise. But each new loss was a blow to us. We never got used to that. The cattle licked at the dry ground, hoping for a scrap of straw. They limped towards us when we brought the hay to feed them. Their loud moo-ing was desperate now.

When I walked the hot mile down to the Henschkes' farm to see Ruth at the end of that afternoon, I found her unusually restless. She couldn't lie still on her bed for one minute but kept tossing about from side to side. She wasn't comfortable. I think her bones hurt her where they pressed on the bed. The tight skin of her face had a strange yellowish tinge. Maybe from the carrots in the night, I thought. The photo of Bernie that I'd brought them was propped up on her dressing-table. He looked so healthy and she looked so sick.

She was as silent as ever. I rushed to fill the silence. I talked on and on to her (or at her) telling her how Miss Playfair had gone home to the city and about Mr Mallorie and the balaclava he was going to knit. I told her how balaclavas go right over your head to keep the cold out.

"And the drought's getting worse," I added with a kind of desperate cheerfulness. "Much much worse. The Murray River's stopped flowing!"

"How do you know?" she demanded, as quick as a flash.

I was startled. Ruth had spoken. I hadn't heard that voice for weeks. It wasn't quite her old voice. It sounded hoarse and strained.

"Dad told me. He heard it from someone in Wally. When he took Miss Playfair to the train. The river-boats up on the Murray are all stranded in the mud along the banks. There's still an inch or two of water in some places but it doesn't move any more."

"Bernie!" she said.

"What about him?"

"No water!"

"Ruth, it's only the Murray that's stopped flowing. Our river's still moving a bit. And so are all the other rivers. They haven't stopped yet."

She made no reply but tossed impatiently onto her other side.

"Do you think Bernie's up on the Murray somewhere?" I asked her. "With your aunties at Swan Hill? Is that what you mean?"

She shook her head.

"I'll have to find him," she whispered.

"Don't be silly! You couldn't walk even half a mile. Your legs'll be all weak from lying in bed. And you're terribly thin. You'd have to get your strength back first."

"I'm not thin!" she said indignantly. Angrily. "Bernie's the thin one! Just look at him!" She stared across at the photo.

I was stunned. Didn't she even know how thin she was?

"Ruth," I said as patiently as I could manage. "That photographer saw Bernie right up near Last Creek. It's a long way from here. Miles and miles. You couldn't possibly go there. Anyway, Bernie said he was moving on. He wasn't staying long at Last Creek. He wouldn't be there any more — even if you went there."

"I'm not going to Last Creek," said Ruth.

"Where are you going then?"

She was silent.

"I'll tell your mother," I threatened, "and she'll tell your Dad!"

"No!" she said and looked back at me with her hollow eyes. I felt frightened.

I didn't actually tell her mother that Ruth was threatening to go off and search for Bernie. I was pretty sure it would come to nothing. Ruth had no strength left at all. She wouldn't get further than the farm gate. But at least she was talking to me now. That was something. I decided to come back every single day to try to keep her talking. I didn't like that bedroom of hers. In fact I hated it. The room was unbearably hot in the day time when the sun was beating down on the iron roof. Even in the evenings it was stuffy. Ruth didn't seem to notice the heat. She even shivered now and then. I couldn't understand it.

Christmas was only a few days off. For once in my life, I wasn't looking forward to it. Without Laurie at home our Christmas would seem empty and without any rain we felt we had nothing to celebrate. I wondered what the Henschkes would be doing about Christmas this year. Their Christmas was always quite different from ours. For one thing, they used to have a Christmas tree. None of the rest of us in the valley ever did that. It wasn't the custom in those days. But Mr Henschke used to go off into the hills with his spade a few days before Christmas and he'd bring back a little wild cherry tree. Its needle-like leaves were dark and soft and glossy. He didn't chop the tree down when he came across it in the bush among the tall gums. He dug it up carefully and carried it back home on his shoulder, roots and all. He planted it in an old kerosene tin packed with good earth and brought it into the house on Christmas Eve. Then twelve days after Christmas, he carried it out again. It was wilting a bit by that time. He planted it in the garden. Sometimes it grew and sometimes it didn't. In the dry years the little tree died off and they had to burn it. But often it recovered well and responded to buckets of water poured lovingly over the roots by Margaret and Mrs Henschke. They had about thirty healthy wild cherry trees, all different sizes, in two rows along the side of their house. The earliest ones went back to the days well before Mr Henschke had been married to Mrs Henschke — the days of his father and mother. That dark green forest gave them a bit of shade in the summer and protected the garden from the worst glare of the sun.

The Henschkes' Christmas tree always used to stand by the window in their front parlour with white candles fixed to its drooping branches. That was one of the few days when they used the front parlour. The puppets and the old violin were taken down from their hooks on the wall. I used to go down to see the tree every year. They really lit the candles. Mother always said it was dangerous. They could set their whole house on fire, she said. I was never there for the whole of Christmas Eve but Ruth told me about it often enough. For her it was the best day of the year — better even than all the birthdays rolled into one. She said that as soon as it was dark they lit the candles on the tree and sang special carols about baby Jesus in the manger and opened up their presents. All that on Christmas Eve! Before we'd even hung up our stockings! Then they sat down to a splendid meal — roast duck or roast chook with fresh herbs in the stuffing. And a glass of wine each, of course. But no Christmas pudding like the ones Mother boiled up in the copper out in our washhouse. I felt that was the one weakness in their marvellous Christmas. The funny thing was that when Christmas Eve was over, the whole of Christmas was more or less over for the Henschkes. They didn't do anything special on Christmas Day. They just got on with their work. And Santa Claus didn't come down their chimney or anything like that. Christmas Eve in the parlour with their wild cherry tree — that was their Christmas celebration, though the green tree stood on in the parlour for twelve more days, dropping its needles onto the bare wooden floor.

That year Mrs Henschke had told Mother that she thought they wouldn't bother with a tree. None of them felt like having the usual happy songs and presents. Two of the boys were at the war; Bernie was lost and Ruth was sick. They didn't want any Christmas at all. I could understand that. I felt much the same myself. But Mother was rather shocked.

"It doesn't seem quite right to me, Char," she said. "I know they don't want a tree but you'd think they'd do something — even if it was just for the little ones. You'd better take something along to Ruth. It's Christmas Eve."

"What could I take?"

"You could make something. A cake?"

"She doesn't eat," I reminded her.

"A nice book-mark?"

I knew Ruth had stopped reading too but I didn't say so.

"All right," I said. "I'll make a book-mark."

You'd probably laugh at my book-mark if you saw it. You wouldn't think it was much of a present for a best friend. But that was the kind of present we gave each other in those days. We didn't buy things — we made them. And they were generally small and simple.

I began with a strip of white card left over from a piece that Miss Playfair had brought with her. I was pretty good at cutting out and colouring after all those evenings with the flags but I certainly didn't draw a Union Jack on Ruth's book-mark. I did flowers and fruits — it reminded me of the Henschkes' garden — and I printed her name and I coloured everything with wax crayons. Then I made a tassle of red silk thread from Mother's embroidery box and tied it on the end. That's all there was to it.

No one was about in the garden when I reached the Henschkes' farm late that afternoon. The cows were gathered round the shed, ready for milking, but there was no sign of Mr Henschke. All our cows were milked already. He was running late, I thought to myself. I knocked on the back door. Fred opened it.

"Hullo Char!" he said. He seemed so glad to see me. "We're all in the front parlour. Come in and see."

I followed him through the kitchen and along the passage to the parlour. I hadn't been in there since the last Christmas Eve. Everything had seemed different then.

The minute I came into the room I could smell the soft resinous scent of a wild cherry tree. There it stood in the window, a taller one than usual, the white candles wired to its branches.

"Oh!" I exclaimed in surprise and pleasure. "You went to get a tree after all! And Ruth!" I cried, suddenly catching sight of her, propped up in an armchair with pillows behind her back. "You're out of bed!"

They all began talking to me at once — the father, the mother and the seven children. Even quiet, serious Margaret was talking. Fred was the one whose voice broke through to me loud and clear.

"Char! Dad didn't go to dig up the tree at all! We found it!

On the verandah! It was lying there when we got up this morning!"

"On the verandah!" I said in astonishment. "How did it get there?"

"We don't know," said Mrs Henschke.

"It was Bernie," said Ruth in her strange cracked voice. She certainly looked much better now she was out of bed and back in the family circle again. Still just as yellowish and still skeleton-thin but with a faint spark of her old liveliness in her eye.

"Bernie!" I said. "How do you know?"

"We don't know, Char," said Mrs Henschke. "All we know is that the tree was there on the verandah this morning. Someone must have put it there in the night. Who could it have been?"

"Mr Mallorie?" I suggested.

"We thought of him," said Mr Henschke. "He's always been kind to us. Always glad to let us have the water from his spring."

"It was Bernie!" said Ruth flatly.

"If it really was Bernie, he can't be far away," I said to Mr Henschke. "Why don't you go out and look for him? Call and shout and coo-ee in the bush?"

"If it's Bernie who brought the tree, we don't need to look for him," Mr Henschke replied. "He wants us to know that he's all right. He'll come home when he's ready. He doesn't want us to worry about him."

"But we can't be sure, Dan," said Mrs Henschke. I could see tears in her eyes.

"I'm sure," said Ruth.

"How would he know it's Christmas?" I asked. "He'd lose all track of time in the bush."

"He'd put a notch in a tree-trunk for every day," said Fred. "In a tree-trunk or in a stick. Just like Robinson Crusoe!"

"We'll light the candles, while Char's here," said Mrs Henschke. "Tom and Harry, you can help me and then you can sing the Christmas hymn for us."

Tom and Harry rushed forward. They lit the candles, one

by one. They sang their little hymn. It was just like their usual Christmas. Or almost. I stayed till the singing was done. I gave Ruth her present.

"I'm sorry," she croaked. "I haven't made you anything."

"That doesn't matter," I said. I was so relieved to hear her talking again and to see her behaving a bit more normally that I certainly wasn't bothered about a present. I wondered if she was going to eat properly but I didn't like to ask.

That half hour by the Henschkes' wild cherry tree was the best part of Christmas for me that year. Our own Christmas Day was almost as dull as I feared it would be. But not quite. Mr Mallorie came in unexpectedly for a plateful of stuffed chook and a slice of Mother's pudding. I cross-examined him straight away.

"Mr Mallorie! Did you leave a wild cherry tree on the Henschkes' verandah? As a kind of present for them?"

He looked genuinely surprised.

"No, lass," he said. "I didn't. Wish I'd thought of it. I know they like them little green trees. Nice thick patch of them they've got there by the house."

"Well, someone brought one. I thought it might've been you."

He shook his head.

"Ruth thinks it could be Bernie," I went on.

"That could be," he said. "I always reckoned the kid wasn't far off, didn't I?"

"Why doesn't he just come home like a sensible boy?" asked Mother. "It's all very peculiar."

"He must've had a bad fright in there at Wally," said Dad. "Something or someone must've scared him. All the same, I wish he'd come back. That family's got quite enough on their minds without worrying about Bernie."

"I'll light up me fire tonight," said Mr Mallorie. "That might draw him back." He pulled out his dirty old pipe and filled it from Dad's tobacco pouch. Dad filled his own. They puffed away together. I liked that smell of burning tobacco. It was comforting.

"I wonder what Miss Playfair's Dad'll make of that

111

marriage certificate," said Mr Mallorie after a long silence. "Look, Alec. I brought it down for you to see for yerself."

He spread the square of yellowing paper on the table. It was creased in both directions with deep folds but the black writing was surprisingly easy to read. There was the bridegroom's name. Mr Mallorie's father. Keith Duncan Mallorie. Carpenter. Free. Then came the bride's name. Mary Isabella Graham. Servant. Free. Then the signature of the minister who married them. The Reverend H. P. Fry, Rector of St George's Parish, Hobart Town. Then the witness. Robert Somerville Playfair. Printer. Free. There was another witness too. She was Free as well. She signed with a cross. The date was the 10th June, 1847.

Dad studied the certificate closely.

"I never knew your Dad had been in Tasmania, Keith," he said. "I thought he lived at Eaglehawk."

"So he did. At least when I was a boy. He must've come across for the gold, I reckon. Or even earlier than that. I was born in 1848 and Eaglehawk's the only place I remember. We might've lived somewhere else first. It's the first I've ever heard about Tasmania as a matter of fact. He never even mentioned it. What was the place called in them days, Alec?"

"Van Diemen's Land," said Dad.

"That's it. No, he never said no word about it. But then he never talked about Scotland neither. He was a silent bloke. Mother was the talker. She told me a lot about 'home' as she used to call the old country. But she never said no word about Hobart Town. Probably they weren't there long. Jist a month or two. The place she loved was Eaglehawk. Missed it terribly when me Dad moved here to settle on the land."

"What's this word 'Free' mean, Mr Mallorie?" I asked. "Look, they're all 'Free'!"

"I dunno," said Mr Mallorie, looking closer. "Funny. I didn't never notice that word before."

"I think I know," said Dad. "It must mean they were all 'Free settlers'. Not convicts. There were lots of convicts over in Tazzy in those early days, you know, Keith. But these characters were all free settlers. Came out in one of those

112

emigrant ships, I daresay. Just like my father — though he came later."

"I hope you're right, Alec," chuckled Mr Mallorie. "Me old Dad was such a stickler for honesty! Belted me if I ever told the slightest fib. Me Dad couldn't never've been an old lag — that's certain. As for me mother — she was a blinking saint! She loved the good old songs and the good old psalms. I used to sing them over to her, Mrs Ross. When she was old."

"Yes. I remember you did. I was just telling Char here the other day, wasn't I, Char?"

I nodded. I wasn't really listening to her. I was thinking about that strange little word. 'Free'. All four of them were 'Free'. 'Free settlers'? I wondered.

9.   Neighbours

Late on Christmas night, Mr Mallorie's fire was burning high on the ridge. I found it oddly comforting to look up from my bedroom window and to see that fire up there — a small splash of orange light against the black sky and the stars. I fell asleep. A few hours later I was suddenly awake. The room was full of moonlight. What had woken me? Too much rich pudding probably. I couldn't settle again so I sat up in bed for a while, the hard iron bars pressing into the small of my back. I fixed my eyes on the distant fire. It was still burning. Was Bernie watching it too, I wondered?

The night was hot and still. My window was pushed up as far as it could possibly go to catch any breath of air. An occasional mopoke called from the roof of our barn.

I stiffened. What was that? Horses on the Track? At this hour? It wasn't possible. All the horses along our valley must surely be safely asleep in their stalls. I listened. But it *was* the sound of horses! Heavy hoofs striking the dry hardened earth. And not just one or two horses either. A mob of them. Had they broken loose from the farms somewhere over the ridge and run blindly into our valley? Or were they wild horses from up in the hills? I'd heard of those wild horses from Grandpa when he was still alive but I'd never been quite sure if they ever existed. Which way were they galloping? Up the Track from Wally or down the Track from the hills? I couldn't tell. How far away? One mile or two? I wasn't sure. There was just the faint but quite distinct thunder of hooves along Gillespie's Track. A strangely menacing sound.

"Well, horses can't hurt us," I told myself as I slid down under the cotton sheet again. "Wherever they've come from,

114

they'll be gone in the morning. I wonder if Dad heard them too?"

One of our own horses neighed loudly from the stables. I fell asleep.

I woke early to find the moonlight gone and the morning sun streaming into my room. Someone was banging and shouting at the back door. It was Fred Henschke's high frightened voice.

"Mr Ross! Mr Ross!"

He was thumping his small fist against our door and shouting Dad's name over and over again.

"Dad!" I called as I jumped out of bed. "It's Fred! Something's wrong!"

Dad had heard him all right. Mother was awake too. All three of us rushed to the back door at the same moment. Dad pulled it open. Fred was there in his nightshirt. No shoes on his feet. He fell in towards us as the door swung wide. Dad caught him and lifted him up in his arms.

"Fred! Fred! What is it?"

"Mr Ross! Char! Please come!" he gasped, struggling in Dad's arms.

"Is it Ruth?" I asked him, grabbing his hand. "Is she dead? Is she dead?"

"No. It's not Ruth. I can't tell you. I can't say it. Come and see!"

He wriggled out of Dad's grasp and ran full tilt out through the door to his horse by the gate. Dad and I dashed to the stables. We ran just as we were in our nightclothes. We unhooked the bridles and slipped them onto the horses' heads but we didn't pause for the saddles.

"Char! You're not dressed!" Mother called after me as Dad and I rode after Fred and down to the Track. She waited only to pull on her own clothes and to snatch up my cardigan. Then she ran to the stables too. She was a good rider. She soon caught us up. The horses all sensed our fear. Their nostrils flared as we galloped. It was such a blue-skied morning. I remember how strange that was — to have such fear in our stomachs on such a beautiful day. The paddocks were brown and the sun brilliantly bright but not yet hot.

Dad and I jumped down by the front gate of the Henschkes' homestead. Fred was there. He was crying and pointing. I saw the window first — the window of the parlour where the Christmas tree stood. A large jagged hole had been ripped from the glass. Broken pieces lay glinting in the sun. Then I saw the garden. Dad gasped.

"No!" he shouted and pushed open the gate.

The garden was in ruins. At the front, at the back and all along the sides of the house. Every single plant had been pulled up by the roots. The potatoes, the carrots and the onions. The beans and the peas. All Margaret's bright flowers. The raspberries and the gooseberries under their nets. They all lay in huge untidy piles like so much rubbish. We walked through the garden all in a dream. A nightmare!

There was worse to come. The lovely fruit trees in the orchard had been cut down — brutally axed to the ground. The apples and the apricots, the walnuts and the mulberries. The little green forest of wild cherry trees, left over from so many Christmases, had been slashed to pieces. Every plant, every bush, every tree in that whole garden lay flat on the dry earth. And just beyond the garden, in the paddock nearest to the house, the vineyard that the Henschkes had been so proud of — all the vines had been wrenched from their wires, their roots dragged bodily from the soil, their green leaves and the bunches of ripening grapes stripped and scattered all over the ground.

The dry taste of fear was rasping in my throat.

"Char! Look at that!" Mother grasped my arm and pointed. I looked. She was staring through the back gate of the garden to the wired enclosure for the chooks and the ducks — the hen house, Mrs Henschke used to call it. It was a terrible sea of still white feathers! Every single bird lay dead, its neck wrung.

"Fred! Where's your father?" demanded Dad as he snapped out of the daze in which we all stood.

"On the floor!" sobbed Fred. "In the kitchen! They're all in there! They're all too scared to come out! And Dad's got his eyes shut. That's why I came to get you. Come on! Come on!"

He pulled Dad back across the yard to the back door.

Dad pushed on the door. It was stuck fast.

"Open up! Open up!" shouted Fred to the family inside. "I've brought Mr Ross!"

Dad pushed harder on the door. I pushed too. It wouldn't budge.

"I climbed out the window," explained Fred. "We've got the table jammed against the door in there. So they couldn't get in."

We heard the sound of voices now and the scraping of the heavy table on the floor. It was being hauled and shoved from the door. Dad rattled on the handle and pushed again. He edged the door open as the table was dragged away.

They were all in there. The whole family — and all in their white nightshirts. Mrs Henschke's hair hung down to her waist. That shocked me almost more than anything else. I'd never seen it like that before. She always wore it in a heavy round bun on her neck. The two little ones, Harry and Tom, were huddled under the dresser. Margaret and Lisa and Kate were still tugging at the table to give us more room to squeeze in. Mrs Henschke was bending over her husband where he lay completely still in the middle of the kitchen floor. As Fred had said, his eyes were shut. The skin around his mouth was blue. Blood was oozing from an ugly swollen gash on his forehead. Ruth stood completely still — her back against the door into the passage — staring out of those gaunt eyes of hers in stunned disbelief.

Dad and Mother knelt down at once by Mr Henschke. Mother pressed her cheek against his heart. She held his wrist..

"He's alive!" she said. "I can hear his heart! He's breathing!"

"How long's he been like this?" asked Dad urgently.

"Half an hour," said Mrs Henschke. She talked fast in short gasps, pushing back the long strands of hair. "He was all right through the whole attack, Mr Ross. He got us all in here and he barricaded the door. He put a wardrobe against the front door too. We locked all the windows. We lit no candles. No lanterns. We just crowded in here and listened to it all. Then

117

at the end they threw a stone in through the parlour window. We heard it smash. That's when we were sure they were coming in to get us. But they didn't. We heard them all laughing. Then they rode off again. We still didn't move an inch. Not for ages. We were afraid they'd be back. Then the first light began to break. We could see each other. We felt safer. Dan said he'd move the table. He stood up. He put his hands out to pull. Then suddenly he let out a cry. He reeled over and fell down to the floor. His head struck the sharp edge of the dresser. That's when I sent Fred to get you, Mr Ross. I thought Dan was dead!"

Mrs Henschke burst into tears. Mother put her arms right around her.

"Oh, Mrs Henschke!" she said. She could find no more words. She was crying now and so was I.

"The first thing is to look after Dan!" said Dad briskly. "I don't know what's happened to him. He could've had a heart attack. In that case it's serious. But it might've just been a faint — from the shock — and then the blow on the dresser knocked him right out."

"Will I make him some tea?" asked Mrs Henschke.

"No, no. Not while he's unconscious. Get a pillow and some blankets. We've got to keep him warm. He might come round."

Mrs Henschke moved Ruth away from the door to the passage and ran for pillows and blankets. She and Mother lifted Mr Henschke's head and eased a pillow underneath. They spread the blankets over his body. Mrs Henschke rubbed his hands between hers.

"Dan! Dan!" she cried. "Come back to us!"

It was as if he had heard her. His eyelids trembled and flickered. His eyes opened. They focussed first on her face and then on the rest of us where we stood, all gazing down at him. Those blue eyes were bewildered. He was slowly remembering the horrors of the night.

"The window!" he said.

Dad nodded. He spoke reassuringly.

"That's it, Dan. Don't you worry. There's a big stone

through the window right enough. But they never got into the house — whoever they were. We can fix up that window in a couple of jiffies."

"The birds!" said Mr Henschke faintly.

Mrs Henschke was crying again.

"We heard them killing the birds!" she sobbed. "It was terrible! The noise! The squawking! The wings beating! We could hear it all from here! My lovely chooks! My ducks too! Are they all dead Mr Ross?"

"I'm afraid so," said Dad. "I'll have to make a fire and burn the lot of them. We can't leave them lying out there in the sun."

"Couldn't we save the feathers?" pleaded Mrs Henschke. "The children could all help me with the plucking. We've lost so much. The garden must be ruined. We could hear the axes — chopping and chopping."

Dad hesitated for a long minute but then he shook his head.

"I don't think you'd better keep the feathers, Mrs Henschke," he said gently. "I know it seems a wicked waste but I don't want you or the children ever to set eyes on that terrible hen house. It's a sight that would haunt you for years. Let me deal with the birds. Then you'll have to face the garden. Just make Dan some tea now. The strongest you've got!"

"Can I help you, Dad?" I offered, hoping he'd say no. He did.

"You stay here with Ruth, Char," he said. "The shock's worst for her. Her strength's the lowest. Keep her warm too."

Dad burnt all the dead birds in a ghastly bonfire of flesh and feathers. The smoke drifted over the house. I led Ruth back to the bed where she'd spent so many listless weeks. I piled the blankets on top of her. I brought her tea. Mother fed the children with bread and butter and set the kitchen to rights again. We all felt better for the hot strong drink.

"Now," said Dad, coming back into the kitchen, his face tense and grim. "I want you all to look at the garden, Mrs Henschke. It's not a pretty sight out there. But it has to be seen. Then we'll decide what to do about it."

Mr Henschke struggled to get up from the floor. He sank back again with a groan.

"Not you, Dan!" said Dad quickly. "Not yet. Emily will stay here with you. But I'd like Mrs Henschke to come. And Margaret. And Ruth."

"Dad!" I protested. "She can't! I've put her on the bed!"

"I think she'll manage. Just drape a blanket round her shoulders. It's a dreadful sight out there but every one of us has to face it. We need to know exactly what's happened. We can't hide away from it. Even Ruth can't hide."

I brought Ruth from the bedroom. She wasn't as reluctant as I was. We left Mother sitting on a chair beside Mr Henschke and we all trailed out of the back door behind Dad. Margaret and Mrs Henschke went first. Then Lisa with Fred and Kate with little Harry and Tom. Ruth and I came last. The sun was shining out there. The magpies were calling. A pair of kookaburras were laughing from a low branch on the gum tree outside the gate. Smoke still hung in the air.

I'll never forget that awful journey we made together around the garden. Dad was relentless. He made us see it all. The vegetables yanked up by the roots; the flowers snapped and scattered; the berry bushes flattened; the fruit trees chopped down; the wild-cherries piled in a dark green mound, the vines in ruins. We all cried then. When we saw the vines. Even Dad cried. That was a shocking sight to me. I'd never seen a man cry before and I've seldom seen it since. He just put one arm round Mrs Henschke's shoulder and he cried. The tears ran down his brown sunburnt cheeks.

"No more! Mr Ross," sobbed Mrs Henschke. "I can't take any more! Let's go in again!"

"There's just one more thing," said Dad. He led us round to the barns. One of the raiders must've found a tin of whitewash in an outhouse. He'd taken a full brush of the stuff and he'd painted a message in large letters right across the door of the barn.

HUNS GO HOME!

We gazed at the words without speaking. Then we turned and walked back with stiff and automatic steps to the house.

"Who did it?" I demanded of anyone and everyone in the kitchen. "Who ever could've done such a thing?"

"It must've been a gang from Wally," said Mother. "They all had horses. They could've come from miles away. They must be strangers."

Mr Henschke spoke from the floor. His colour had come back a bit.

"No!" he said. "I heard the voices. And I heard them calling each other. I didn't know them all. But some of them I did know. They were the neighbours' kids! Donny Pollock was one of them. And Jim and Dave Morison. And Stu Douglas. And even young Jeff Logan. And a lot of men. I don't know who they were. They kept quiet. Neighbours from further up the valley, I suppose."

"Neighbours!" gasped Mrs Henschke.

"What's happening to this country?" asked Mother.

"It's the war!" said Dad. "The war's driven everyone mad!"

"We can't stay here, Dan," said Mrs Henschke. "We'll have to move. We'll have to go up to my sisters in Swan Hill."

"We're staying!" said Mr Henschke. "We'll plant the garden again."

"But the fruit trees!" she cried. "And the vines! They've been growing for years and years! We can't start all over again!"

"We'll plant new trees!" said Mr Henschke from the floor. His voice was strong now. "And we'll plant new vines!"

"Dad!" cried a strangled voice from the back door. We all swung round. It was Bernie!

10. The Knack

Ruth stumbled across the kitchen towards Bernie. His eyes widened in sudden shock as he caught sight of her gaunt face and her skinny arms.

"Ruth!" he cried. "What ever's happened to you?"

She didn't answer. She just gripped his brown wrists in a fierce claw-like grasp.

"She's been ill, Bernie!" I gabbled. "But now you're back I'm sure she'll soon get better. She was so worried about you! She was desperate! We've all been desperate! Why on earth did you run off like that?" My voice sounded angrier than I meant it to be. I wanted to sound kind.

"Sorry, Char," he said. "I just had to run! I was scared. I got three letters in there at Wally."

"Who from?" asked Dad.

"I don't know, Mr Ross. But they got worse and worse. First they said I was a bloody Hun. I didn't mind that too much. Then they said they'd kill me. I began to feel frightened. Then they said they'd kill all of you — the whole stinking Bosch family, they said — if I didn't get right out of Wally. So I got right out! I thought if I disappeared completely they'd leave you alone. I was wrong about that."

"You should've come straight home, son," said Mrs Henschke.

"No! They said if I tried to come home they'd be sure to follow me. They'd get us all in one go, they said! They reckoned they'd burn the whole place down and kill our stock, and finish us off! They hate us, Mum! Don't you know that? They hate us!"

"But how did you live, Bernie?" I asked. "What did you eat?" That was the question that had puzzled me for weeks. I had to ask it now.

Bernie laughed a short laugh.

"There's lots to tell you about that, Char. I ate some peculiar things out there in the bush. But I survived."

"Were you far from here?" asked Ruth.

"Not far in the end. I began my run in another valley altogether. Up near a place called Last Creek. That was a fair way off. But then I somehow wanted to move back towards home. It was crazy, I suppose. I just couldn't keep away. So I made myself a camp up there on the ridge on the wild side of the river. I built a shelter from some branches. Not that I needed much shelter. When I climbed a tree up there, I could look right down here onto the farm. I thought I could see you in the garden, Mum. And at night I sometimes used to see a fire over by Mr Mallorie's hut. I liked that. It made me feel better. I slept a lot in the day time and then at night I'd come down the hill to watch Gillespie's Track from the far side of the river. Just to make sure no mob was coming to attack you. Then last night I did see them coming. Twenty of them at least, riding up the Track on their horses. There was quite a moon shining. Very bright and clear. I saw them as plain as day. It was too late to warn you. They were almost at the farm by the time I'd spotted them."

"What did you do?" I asked him.

"I crept across the river here — there's hardly any water left in it. And I hid in the scrub only about a hundred yards or so from the house. So I saw it all. I watched them wrecking our garden. But I was too scared to move at first. Then when they started on the fruit trees I just tore back over the river and up to the top of the wild ridge." He turned towards Mr Henschke. "Dad, I've often thought how I'd save you all. I'd planned it out in the bush. But I was terrified! I'm sorry! I just ran away!"

For one awful minute I was afraid Bernie was going to cry. His face looked strange. Then he pulled himself together.

"I'm sorry, Dad," he said again.

"Thank goodness you didn't try to save us, Bernie!" cried Mrs Henschke. "You could've been killed!"

"Who were they, son?" asked Mr Henschke, looking up at him from the floor, a frown pulling his eyebrows together. "Could you see them at all? Did you know them?"

"Some I thought I knew. All the local boys were there. The boys I knew at school. Stu Douglas and Jim and Dave Morison. And Donny Pollock. Some of their Dads were with them. Mr Pollock from the store was one of them. And Mr Morison. And Mr Logan. I didn't see Mr Douglas. He could've been there."

"Not Ron Morison, surely!" exclaimed Dad in astonishment. Bernie nodded.

"He was there all right. But some of the other men I didn't know. Farmers from down the valley, I suppose, or blokes from Wally."

None of us spoke for a minute or two.

"What a terrible end to Christmas!" I said at last.

"But Bernie's back!" said Ruth. "That's something!"

"We'd better go home," said Mother. "Char! You're not even dressed!" She knew that already but she suddenly seemed to notice it again.

"Come up and have something to eat with us," said Dad. "At the end of the morning. There's enough food, isn't there, Em?"

"Plenty," said Mother, brightening. "We'd like that. Do come, Mrs Henschke. Soon after twelve."

"And then we'll talk about all this," said Dad, waving his hand towards the devastation beyond the kitchen window.

"But Mr Henschke can't get up!" I said.

"Yes, I think I can, Char. That giddiness has gone. Give me a hand there, Bernie. I'm glad you're home, son. We need you here."

Bernie and Dad each took one of Mr Henschke's arms and raised him first to a sitting position and then to his feet. He swayed slightly and then stood firm. He put one hand up to the cut to his head. He winced.

"Sleep!" he said to Mrs Henschke. "That's what we all

need, Katherine. A few hours of solid sleep. Then we can tackle anything."

"Don't forget the cows, Dad," said Bernie. "They haven't been milked."

Mr Henschke groaned.

"I did forget the cows," he said.

"We'll all help," said Margaret, the quiet one. "You needn't do the cows, Dad. You go to bed."

Mother and Dad and I left them. We walked slowly through the ruined garden. We looked across the fence at the smouldering fire and the wreck of the vineyard. Our horses were still standing patiently in a patch of shade outside the front gate. We rode home again.

"You'd better sleep too, Char," said Dad, looking at me. "I'll do the milking on my own this morning. I'll just take my time."

I was glad he said that. I flung myself straight onto the bed. When I woke again the Henschkes were all trooping through the back door — even Mr Henschke himself with a white bandage round his head.

"Where's Ruth?" I asked.

"She's coming in the buggy," said Fred. "She couldn't walk all that way, Char. Bernie's driving her. He's piled lots of pillows in the buggy. So her bones won't hurt."

I heard the wheels of the buggy and ran out to meet them. Mr Mallorie was just shuffling through the back gate. We didn't know he was coming too! All fourteen of us somehow squashed around our kitchen table. Mum had cooked a whole new Christmas dinner! It tasted far better than the one the day before. Dad carved the roast mutton. A whole huge leg to feed such a multitude. I dished up the potatoes and Mother did the cabbage.

"Do you want to eat anything, Ruth?" I asked, hesitating with the spoon in my hand.

"Just a skerrick," she said, smiling at me. Her face was as haggard as ever but something of her old spirit was coming back again. I gave her the tiniest portion.

Bernie talked through most of that meal on Boxing Day. At

last I found out what he'd been eating in the bush! He'd had the good sense to take plenty of matches with him when he'd run off from Wally so he could always make a fire to cook what he caught. He had an old black billy and his rabbit trap and his fishing line. That was enough, he said. Baked rabbits and eels. Boiled bracken and nettles. I shuddered.

"What about water?" I asked.

"I stuck close to the creeks," he said.

"But they're all drying up!" I said.

"I know. One of my creeks dried up completely. I couldn't find another. So I had to dig for water. I found a little spring."

"How?" asked Mr Mallorie, looking across the table at him sharply.

Bernie paused a minute or two. It seemed to me that he didn't want to say any more.

"With a forked twig," he said at last. "I met a photographer bloke early on. He showed me how to do it. I didn't believe him at first. But it works all right. If you've got the knack of it."

"What do you mean, Bernie?" asked Mrs Henschke.

"I'll show you, Mum. I just hold the two arms of the forked stick between my hands. When I walk over water, the end points down. It sort of swings."

"I don't believe it!" said Mr Henschke.

"I do," said Mr Mallorie. "I've seen me old Dad doing jist that. Back in the early days. At Eaglehawk. I was telling you, Char, wasn't I?"

I nodded.

"Well, laddie," Mr Mallorie went on, turning back to Bernie. "It's jist as well you've got that knack. Me spring's dried up this morning. We're going to need your forked twig right here in this valley."

"Dried up?" exclaimed Mother. "Surely not, Mr Mallorie. Char filled our buckets there yesterday."

"A trickle yesterday, Mrs Ross," he said. "And nothink today."

"But Bernie. That twig'll never work," his father persisted.

"Yes it will, Dad. It'll just have to work. Our river's pretty well stopped running now. I took the horses down there for a drink this morning. When you were all asleep. It's just a long muddy puddle now. It doesn't move. I dropped a leaf onto the water and I watched for half an hour. It never moved an inch."

"Our river?" exclaimed Dad. "Stopped running? Like the Murray?"

"Yep," said Bernie matter-of-factly. He didn't sound as worried as we all were. He hadn't had to watch the sheep and cattle dying off for weeks.

"You'd better find your twig this afternoon, laddie," said Mr Mallorie, as pleased as punch with the whole desperate situation. "I seen it work when I was a boy and now I reckon I'll see it again. You jist find the place, laddie, and we'll dig the hole, won't we, Alec?"

Dad looked unconvinced.

"I've never heard of it," he said. "I don't believe in it. But we'll have to try it. We've got no choice."

"What sort of twig, Bernie?" I asked.

"Wattle's best. It's springy. But anything will do."

"Come on, Bernie! Come on! Let's get started!" I cried, jumping up in my place. I was wildly excited.

"Eat your rice pudding first, Char!" said Mother firmly. "The water can wait."

After the meal we all went out into the blistering afternoon heat with Bernie. He found a light wattle branch, forked at one end. He cut it from the tree and stripped off the feathery leaves. It was just about two feet long. A bit more than a twig, I thought to myself.

"Where will you look, Bernie?" I asked as we all stood round him, pushing in close to see his slender stick.

"On your Dad's land first, Char. Well up this hill a bit. Those springs of water are often under the steep slopes."

"Quite right," agreed Mr Mallorie. "Jist the same at Eaglehawk."

He shuffled twice as fast as usual and kept up easily with the rest of us as we made our way up the hill. His excitement pushed him along. He clutched tighter to his trouser legs, just above the knees.

Dad and Mr Henschke walked slowly at the back. They carried the spades but they were pretty suspicious about the whole thing.

"Never heard of it, Dan," Dad muttered from time to time.

Half way up the ridge we came to a halt. We sat in the shade of a clump of gums to leave Bernie in peace to try out his twig. I looked down along the whole dry valley spread out below us. There were the empty dams. There was the muddy streak of river. In another day or two of heat like this even those shallow water-holes along the river bed could be gone. The sun was sucking the valley dry. If Bernie didn't find any water, we'd have to shoot the rest of the livestock. We'd have to leave the farm. Just like the Craiks. I sighed. I only half believed in Bernie's twig.

He began his search. We all sat still and watched him. He held the two prongs of the wattle branch lightly between his big hands. The sharp end pointed straight ahead of him. Slowly he walked across the parched ground. Twenty yards away from us and then twenty yards back again. Up the hill a few paces. Then twenty yards away and twenty yards back again. Still the stick pointed forwards.

"I knew there was nothing in it!" said Mr Henschke. "This is a wild-goose chase."

"Be patient, Dan," said Mrs Henschke. "Give the boy a fair go. He's only just started."

"Could take hours," said Mr Mallorie. "I seen it take hours."

So we sat on together and waited. Bernie combed that part of the side of our hill, inch by inch. We kept our eyes fixed on him all the time. I began to lose hope.

"Hey!" shouted Bernie suddenly. He'd stopped in his tracks.

We stared at him! The twig was moving! Slowly it swung downwards. It was pointing at the dry leaves on the ground.

"Dig here!" cried Bernie. "Dig here!"

Dad grabbed his spade and ran to the spot to dig. I took the other spade from Mr Henschke's hands and gave it to Bernie. The two of them pushed their spades into the rock-hard earth and stamped on them to force them down. It was slow hot work. The soil they threw up showed not a hint of moisture. We all pressed close and watched them. The sweat poured off Dad's forehead.

"Give me a go now, Alec," said Mr Mallorie. He was a good digger, Mr Mallorie. His arms were better than his weak old legs. He joined Bernie in their hole. It was about three feet deep.

Mr Henschke was shaking his head from side to side as he watched them.

"Come back to the shade, Dan," said Mrs Henschke. "This sun's not good for you. Not after that knock you had, dear."

"Look!" shouted Mr Mallorie. He threw away his spade and bent down into the hole. He rubbed his hand on the earth at the very bottom. He held up his hand for all of us to see. It was smeared with dark red mud.

"It's wet!" he cried.

He took up the spade again and attacked the ground with a flood of new excitement and energy. The three youngest Henschkes crouched close to the hole and stared in. Ten minutes later Bernie paused. Mr Mallorie stopped digging. They stepped up out of their hole. We all leant over and peered in. Slowly but surely, water was seeping into the bottom. It was a spring! Bernie had found water!

Dad was astounded.

"Well done, lad!" he said. "I never thought you'd do it. We'll have to dig deeper but there's water flowing here all right."

The digging went more easily now. We all took a turn. Even Margaret. In fact she was used to digging from the garden but this hole was rather different. Mother had a go for a few minutes and Mrs Henschke too. No one wanted to be left out. The little ones scrabbled in the hole with the trowels they'd brought. All of us felt happy. The horrors of the night and the devastated garden seemed forgotten for an hour. I filled my cupped hands with the cool new water and flung it up into Bernie's face. Bernie laughed. Everyone laughed.

"You'd better find us a spring on our own farm now, son," said Mr Henschke.

"And another by my hut too!" added Mr Mallorie.

Bernie smiled in triumph.

"I've had an idea about the garden, Dad," he said.

"What?"

"Some of those vegies they've ripped up will store quite well in the barn if we get them in quick — the potatoes and the onions and the carrots. Then we could spread out all the rest and all the fruit in the sun to dry. Even the grapes — they're almost ripe and they'd dry to raisins. When everything's good and dry, we can store it all in the barn too. That'll give us food for weeks. Months. While we're waiting for the garden to grow again."

"I can't eat dried-up food, Bernie!" protested Fred.

"You don't have to eat it dry! Mum cooks it in water and it goes all soft again."

I thought that was a brilliant idea. Bernie was definitely the cleverest person I'd ever known. Cleverer even than Dad. Cleverer than Miss Playfair! Dad liked the drying suggestion too.

"Good plan, Bernie," he said. "And I'll go into Wally with the buggy in a day or two to buy up new seeds for the garden. And new chicks for the hen house too," he added, looking at Mrs Henschke. He turned to Mr Henschke. "Best not go into Wally yourself, Dan. Only asking for trouble from the hooligans in there. Hooligans and larrikins they are. Just leave me to do the buying."

"Thanks, Alec," said Mr Henschke. "When the season's right, we'll want some new vines too and some little fruit trees."

Dad nodded.

Bernie's plan worked well. I helped Mrs Henschke and Margaret to spread six huge white sheets from their linen cupboard out in the backyard. Both families came together in the cool of the evening to scatter the fruit and vegetables over the sheets. Each day the sun beat down on the sheets and dried the grapes and the nuts and the soft fruit and all the vegies. Bernie turned everything over every day. I liked to come and help him whenever Dad could spare me — though that wasn't often. When all was dry and light, the Henschkes stacked it away in their barn. They weren't going to starve, anyway.

Ruth had begun to eat again. She never tried big helpings but she managed a little bit more each day. She even sat at the table with all the rest of the family at meal time. Her face was losing that strange yellowish colour. She was filling out again. Her arms were less like sticks. She was almost her old self again now that Bernie was home.

I felt different too though I'm not sure why. Perhaps it was the water. The new spring Bernie had found for us on the hillside gave us plenty of water for our stock and plenty for the house. It never stopped flowing though the drought got worse. There was no more grass for the sheep or the cows. Our hay had all gone so we had to buy fodder to feed them. We managed to save some of them though we couldn't save them all.

Bernie took his forked twig up to Mr Mallorie's hut but he didn't find a drop of water anywhere on the top of the ridge. Mr Mallorie just had to fill his buckets at our new water-hole every day. And on the Henschkes' own farm, Bernie uncovered three good springs. It was just as well he did. Ten days after Christmas the river had gone completely dry. Bernie's springs saved our farm and the Henschkes'. We were lucky. The other families at Deepwater weren't so lucky. They were desperate. The Pollocks at the store and all the farmers — the Douglases, the Logans and the Morisons — they didn't have a bucket of water between the lot of them.

The neighbours had heard, of course, about Bernie's twig. Straight away they'd tried the same kind of thing themselves but without success. They began to see it wasn't just the twig that found the water — it was the person who held the twig. Not everyone had the knack that Bernie had. So one hot afternoon in the middle of January, a little knot of embarrassed farmers gathered on the Henschkes' front verandah. They all held their hats in their hands. Their faces seemed stiff. They tried not to look to right or to left at the ruined garden where Margaret and Mrs Henschke were digging and planting and watering. Ruth came to the door. She told me all about it. They asked for her father. He came out of the house. He looked at the men.

"Dan," said Mr Morison. "We've come to say we're sorry. About all this." He jerked one elbow towards the garden. "We never should've let the boys do that. We knew where they were off to that night and we should've stopped them. We shouldn't have joined in. We don't know what got into us. We must've been mad. Some of those blokes from the town egged us on but we never should've listened to them. We're sorry, Dan."

Mr Henschke made no reply.

"I would've sent them all packing!" I said angrily to Ruth.

"Dad's not like that," she said.

"It's water we're needing, Dan," Mr Morison had gone on. "We've heard about that boy of yours. He's got a way with water. We were wondering . . ." and he hesitated for a minute. "We were just wondering if young Bernie could lend us a hand, like. With that twig of his."

"Yes," said Mr Henschke. "Bernie'll help you."

"Dad!" protested Bernie who'd come out to stand beside him. "I won't! Just look what they did to us! They think we're huns! I'll never help them!"

"Off you go, son. Take your wattle twig with you. Our neighbours need water. You've got the knack. We can't refuse. People on the land have to stick together in hard times. You know that."

Bernie was reluctant but he took his twig and went. He found nine springs altogether on the farms at Deepwater and three more at Kanyul. Before long the men at Talisker and Burnett's Bridge and Longstone Bend were sending for him too. Bernie was famous. He searched that whole valley along Gillespie's Track with his wattle twig. The water was there all right. But it was hidden. Deep under the ground. Only Bernie Henschke seemed to have the knack of finding it.

11. Free!

Early in February, Miss Playfair was back with us at Deepwater for the start of the new school year. She settled into her old room off our verandah as if she'd never been away. After all those weeks living with her father down in the city, she had plenty to talk about. The war, for example. She knew all about it. Her father said the boys wouldn't be going straight off to France from that camp by the pyramids. No. First they'd be going to fight the Turks, over near the Dardanelles. She'd brought a brand-new map to show us and she spread it out on the kitchen table. Certainly it didn't look very far to me across the strip of blue sea from Egypt. Only a couple of inches on the map.

Miss Playfair's father was going to post *The Argus* up to her from the city every single day now. From that time onwards she didn't have to rely on his letters or his sheafs of cuttings or the occasional front page to keep herself up to date with the war. She could read the whole paper for herself. She could read it aloud to us in the kitchen before tea. She could read it to the children in the school. And she did. I was never sure if Mother really enjoyed those readings in the kitchen as she bent over the stove. Of course, she did want to know something about the war but when she had to listen every day to the same headlines about fierce battles in France and Belgium, I rather think she wanted to block up her ears.

Mr Mallorie had called in only a day or two after Miss Playfair's return from the city. She was reading the war news to us at the time. He came quietly into the kitchen without even knocking and sat down in an empty chair, waiting till she'd finished.

"Well read, Miss!" he exclaimed when she finally put the paper aside.

"Oh, Mr Mallorie!" she said, pink with pleasure at his words. "I've brought your stone safely back again. I'll just get it for you."

She glided to her bedroom and brought the stone, carefully wrapped in layer upon layer of white tissue paper.

"I didn't want it to get damaged," she explained as she unwrapped all those soft coverings. The stone emerged at last. Mr Mallorie almost snatched at it and held it tightly in his two gnarled hands.

"I shouldn't never've let it go, Miss," he said. "I haven't felt quite meself without it, you know. Had this funny feeling of somethink missing. All over Christmas. Somethink missing."

"I'm so sorry," she said seriously.

"I'd do best to have it buried with me, I reckon," he said.

She seemed to approve of that idea. She nodded and smiled.

"And what did yer Dad think of it? Did he take it to the museum like I said?"

"No. He was too busy really. He didn't have the time. But I took it myself, Mr Mallorie."

Mr Mallorie leant forward.

"And what did they say?" he asked.

"They were most interested," she said. "They kept it there all day. I had to go back at five o'clock just before they locked up. They showed me these tiny little scratches through a magnifying glass. 'Chatter-marks' they're called. The stones roll together on the beach under the waves. They make a chattering sound as they scrape against each other."

"But where did it come from?" I persisted.

"They said the grey flint could come from anywhere — or anywhere there's flint about, I mean," said Miss Playfair. "But the little orange pebble that's wedged inside. That's quite rare. There's only one place in Australia where you find pebbles just like that."

"Where?" I asked.

"In Tasmania. On the stony beaches round Barracks Bay. It's a sea-stone, they told me. Not a river-stone."

"Barracks Bay?" said Mr Mallorie. "I've never heard of that, Alec, have you?"

Dad shook his head.

"My father hadn't heard of it either," said Miss Playfair. "But then we don't really know Tasmania. It's like another country almost, isn't it?"

"And the marriage lines, Miss? What did he make of that?"

Miss Playfair gave such a violent start of surprise that I wondered if she was putting it on.

"Oh!" she exclaimed. "I'm so sorry! I forgot all about that marriage certificate, I'm afraid. I didn't ever show it to my father."

"Never mind, Miss. Never mind," said Mr Mallorie quickly but he looked disappointed. "I jist thought yer Dad might've been able to explain it to me a bit. He sounds like a clever man, yer Dad."

"He is!" said Miss Playfair earnestly.

"I've had me own idea about that word 'Free', Miss. I been thinking it over all through Christmas."

"It's 'Free settler', Keith," said Dad. "I told you."

"Could be, Alec. Could be. But I had this new idea. It could be 'Free to marry'! How's that, now? Not married already! Free to marry! Same as 'bachelor' and 'spinster'."

"No, Mr Mallorie! That can't be it," I said at once.

"Why not, lass?"

"Well, I can see your father and mother had to be free to marry. They were getting married to each other that day. But what about Miss Playfair's grandfather? Robert Somerville Playfair? He was just the witness. He didn't need to be free to marry, did he? But he's got 'Free' beside his name. And so's that other witness too. I forget what she was called."

"Ann Lewis," said Mr Mallorie. "She jist made her mark, as we used to say in the early days. Yes, she was 'Free' too."

"'Free settlers'!" said Dad. "That's the only answer!"

"I'm sure you're right, Mr Ross," said Miss Playfair firmly. "That's what my father would be sure to think too."

"I wish I knew for certain, Miss," said Mr Mallorie, scratching his head.

"I must get my things ready for school tomorrow," said Miss Playfair, rolling up her splendid new map of the war.

The younger Henschke children were all back at school that term. Lisa and Kate, Fred and Harry. There seemed to be an unspoken agreement between the farmers at Deepwater and Kanyul that their kids at the school would leave the Henschkes in peace. No more teasing. No more taunting. No more words like Hun and Bosch and Fritz flung across the playground. No more icy silence. Miss Playfair made no comment at all on the Henschkes' reappearance. She simply absorbed them back into her school without a word.

Ruth didn't go back to school with the others. For one thing, she wasn't nearly strong enough yet. For another thing, she said she felt too old. More important, she wanted to begin to help Bernie on the farm. To my astonishment — and hers — Mr Henschke agreed. He went against the habits of a lifetime.

"Charlotte Ross has come to no harm helping her Dad, as far as I can see," he said to Ruth. "She's a good lass. Her face is a bit too brown but she's nice and lady-like. Bernie and I certainly need another pair of hands. We've got to plant the trees and the vines and we've got all the other work too. I'd sooner have you than someone from outside the family. So when you've filled out and found your strength again, you can start."

She began by pottering in the garden, carrying water for Margaret. It was April before she could really be much use to Bernie on the farm. Mother was pleased when Ruth started at last. I wasn't the only girl in the valley getting filthy on the land. I think she must have thought that two old hags would be better than just one!

Mr Mallorie had to come right down to our spring to fill his buckets now just as we used to go up to his. He liked to come early in the morning. Often I didn't see him at all. I was in the milking shed. But now and then we happened to meet at the spring and I'd help him to carry the buckets up the hill. I prided myself on being able to carry a full iron bucket right to his hut without spilling a single drop. Water was too precious to waste.

"Now, lass," he said to me one dry windy morning in March when we'd put the two buckets in the shade of a tree by his door. "Could you jist step inside for a minute? I need some help. I'm writing a letter."

"Mother said you can write well," I said.

"I can copy things, lass, real good. But I'm not so quick with the making-up. It's the spelling, you see."

I followed him into his hut. I'd never been inside before. Chinks of light shone in between the logs. Everything was tidy and ship-shape, just the way his mother had taught him to keep it years ago.

"It's that marriage certificate, you know, lass. I want to write off and find out more."

"Who to?" I asked.

"To the Rector." He picked up the certificate from beside his bed and read from it slowly. "The Rector of St George's parish, Hobart Town."

I laughed out loud.

"But Mr Mallorie!" I protested. "That man's been dead for years and years! He signed the certificate in 1847! This is 1915!"

Mr Mallorie looked pained.

"I'm not so stupid as you think, lass. I'm not writing to *this* Rector! Not to this Reverend H. P. Fry! I'm writing to the *present* Rector! He'll have all his church records in some cupboard down there. He can tell me about that word 'Free'."

"How do you know there's still a rector?"

"Must be," he said. "A whole church can't disappear. Churches last for hundreds and hundreds of years. They're made of stone, lass. If there's a church, there'll be a Rector. A Reverend."

"Well, all right. What do you want to say to him?"

Mr Mallorie was so pleased. He produced paper and pen and ink.

"Dear Sir," he began firmly.

I wrote to his dictation, improving the grammar a bit as I went.

Dear Sir,

I've got here the marriage certificate of my parents, Keith Duncan Mallorie and Mary Graham. They were married in your church on 10th June 1847 by the Reverend H. P. Fry. There were two witnesses — Robert Somerville Playfair and Ann Lewis. They were all 'Free'. What is the meaning of 'Free'?

Yours faithfully,

Mr Mallorie signed the letter himself, in large round writing, Keith Graham Mallorie. Slowly he added his address, High Hut, Deepwater, Gillespie's Track, Victoria.

"He mightn't ever answer, Mr Mallorie," I warned him. I wanted to save him from disappointment.

"Never mind, lass. It's worth a try. If the rector don't answer, I'll try the Public Library. I want to find out."

"Sometimes it's best not to find out," I said.

"The truth can't never hurt us, lass," he said. "That's what me old mother always said."

I wasn't so sure. But I addressed the letter for him to the Rector of St George's Parish Church, Hobart, Tasmania. Mr Mallorie counted out his pennies for a stamp. I posted the letter that very morning at the store.

In the warm light evenings of March and early April, I often wandered down to the Henschkes' farm after tea to talk to Ruth and Bernie. We talked about our farm and their farm. We talked about the drought. We talked about the lambing and the lambs born dead. We talked about the low yield of milk and the new losses of stock. We didn't mention the war. I'd rather given up helping Miss Playfair with her War Book. Anyway, she wasn't quite so interested in it herself. Mother said she spent all her evenings shut away in her room, writing letters. She didn't sit on in the kitchen any more.

Miss Playfair still received a lot of letters too. More than ever, in fact. Mother collected them along with ours when she called in at the Post Office in the store. Laurie didn't write often to us but someone in Egypt was writing to Miss Playfair and it wasn't Laurie. We knew Laurie's handwriting. The writing on her letters was quite different and the ink was green. The sender's name was never printed on the outside so although I studied the envelopes and the stamps very carefully before Miss Playfair came in from school, I could never discover who had sent them.

"It could easily be one of her cousins," said Mother, who didn't like the way I pried at the letters where they waited on the mantelpiece, "or an old school friend from her High School days. It won't be anyone we know, Char, so leave those letters alone. It's very rude to turn them over and over like that."

Each afternoon, when Miss Playfair came in after school, hot from the long walk up the hill from our gate in all the heat, her eyes went at once to the mantelpiece. When no letters were there, she tried to hide her disappointment by talking busily about the school. When a letter *was* there, she flushed scarlet at once. She took it straight to her bedroom and closed the door. She stayed inside for ages and ages.

"Whoever he is, he must write terribly long letters!" I said to Mother one afternoon. "She's been reading it now for more than an hour!"

Mother laughed.

"She's probably reading it over and over, Char. That's what you do with a love-letter. If it *is* a love-letter, I mean. You read it till you know it off by heart."

"Huh!" I scoffed. "That's crazy, Mother. I'd never do a thing like that!"

Mother just smiled.

When Miss Playfair finally came out to have her tea, I sometimes thought she looked as if she'd been crying. I did feel sorry for her then. I hoped he hadn't said unkind things to her — this unknown soldier in Egypt.

Then one Friday early in April the amazing secret was out! There wasn't just a letter waiting for her on the mantelpiece that afternoon. There was a small square packet, plastered with red Egyptian stamps. For once Miss Playfair didn't slip off to her room as usual but sat down at the table and opened up the packet in front of us all.

Inside the tough brown paper was a tiny black box. Inside the box was white cotton-wool. Then out of the cotton-wool rolled a bright gold ring!

"I'm engaged!" said Miss Playfair, turning pink with triumph and happiness as she slipped the ring onto the fourth finger of her left hand and gazed down at the greenish Egyptian stone set deep in the gold. "Engaged to be married!"

"Who to?" I asked bluntly.

"Char!" said Mother. "That's Miss Playfair's business! Not yours!"

"Oh, it's quite all right, Mrs Ross. I don't mind telling you at all. I've wanted to tell you for weeks. Now the ring's here, I can speak out at last. It's someone you know!"

"Not Laurie!" gasped Mother, trying to hide her alarm. I don't think she wanted Laurie to marry anyone!

"No, no!" laughed Miss Playfair. "It's not Laurie. It's Colin Douglas!"

"Col!" Mother and I exclaimed together.

"But you've never ever met him, Miss Playfair," I said. "He'd gone off to the war before you came to Deepwater!"

"That's true, Charlotte," she said calmly. "But Colin and I have written so many letters to each other, you see. I was the first to write. Soldiers long for letters. I couldn't write to them all so I just picked one. I picked Colin. And now I feel I know him very well. I have his photograph and he has mine. We feel exactly the same about everything. The war has brought us together."

Her eyes were shining.

Miss Playfair took the gold locket that hung around her neck and opened it up. On one side was a tiny photo of a soldier in uniform. We looked closely. It was Col all right. On the other side was a fierce whiskery gentleman with sharp eyes. Not the same as the one of her father in her bedroom, I thought.

"My grandfather," she explained. "My father likes me to wear it."

"Well!" said Mother, pulling herself together. "We wish you every joy, Miss Playfair. Col Douglas is a fortunate young man. We hope you'll be very happy. And when will the wedding be?"

"After the war," she said. "That can't be long now. When Colin comes back home."

"*If* he comes back home!" I thought to myself.

"And will you live in our valley, Miss Playfair?" I asked her. "On the Douglases' farm?"

She nodded.

I was surprised to find that I was no longer quite so keen to have her living in our valley. I didn't even care about being a bridesmaid. Strange how feelings can change.

Mr and Mrs Douglas heard the news the same day as we did. They had a letter from Col. They rode across at once to visit Miss Playfair and to say how delighted they would be to have her as their daughter-in-law. They even wanted her to move to their farmhouse straight away but she said she thought she'd like to stay on with us for the time being.

"The war will soon be over, Mrs Douglas," she said, "and then Colin and I can be married."

I noticed the way she rolled the words 'Mrs Douglas' off her tongue. I think she liked the sound of them. She'd soon be 'Mrs Douglas' herself.

"You're probably right, my dear," said Mrs Douglas, looking with admiration at Miss Playfair's smoothly coiled hair and her lovely white tucked blouse.

"And what does your father say to all this, Miss Playfair?" asked Mr Douglas. "Course, you couldn't do better than our Col, though I say it myself. He's a good lad! But your father's never met him, has he? You've never met him yourself!"

"Colin wrote my father such a nice letter," said Miss Playfair, "asking for his consent. My father gave it straight away, of course. He said we couldn't possibly refuse a brave young soldier who's fighting for King and Country!"

"True enough," said Mr Douglas, nodding with approval. "Mind you, our Col's a bit headstrong. Can be difficult now and then. But I'm sure you'll tame him, Miss Playfair."

She smiled contentedly to herself.

"Char," said Mother a few days later as I came into the kitchen half way through the afternoon for a drink of water.

"Mmm?" I said, sipping the cool water slowly.

"Mr Mallorie was asking for you. He wants you to go up

141

and see him today."

"I can't go till I've finished the work with Dad. We've got more dead lambs. What did he want?"

"I don't know," said Mother. "He didn't say."

I had to wait till well after five o'clock before Dad could let me go. I half ran up the hill to High Hut. I was pretty sure what Mr Mallorie wanted me for. He must've had an answer from the Rector of St George's.

I was right. The letter was propped up on his mantelpiece, just the way we propped ours. It was next to his mother's clock.

"It's come, lass!" he said, rubbing his hands together in excitement. "I collected it this morning. But I haven't opened it. I wanted to wait till you was here. I feel too nervous-like to see it on me own. Here! You read it out to me! Your eyes are quicker than mine!"

I slit the envelope and I took out the letter. I opened it up and read aloud.

Dear Mr Mallorie,

Thank you for your letter. Unfortunately the Rector is ill at present. He has passed your letter on to me. I have consulted our marriage registers here at St George's for 10th June, 1847. I find, indeed, that your parents were married here on that day by the Reverend H. P. Fry. What is still more interesting is that the two witnesses at your parents' wedding, Robert Somerville Playfair and Ann Lewis, were themselves married on that same day. Your own parents were the witnesses to their wedding.

Now for the word 'Free'. As it happens, I have a keen amateur interest in the early records of Tasmania and I am familiar with the use of this word. Most of the brides and bridegrooms married by the Reverend H. P. Fry were described as 'Free', though some were described as 'PH', Pass Holder. The word 'Free' was applied to former convicts who had completed their full sentence of transportation, generally of seven years, and who had been granted their 'Free Certificate'. This meant that they were free to follow any employment or even to leave the colony of Van Diemen's Land and cross to Port Phillip District, now Victoria.

I have consulted the convict archives in our Hobart library to see what further information I could give you about your parents. I assume you would prefer to know the full truth of their crimes. I am glad to tell you that the matter was not serious. Both were transported for petty larceny — that is for stealing. In your father's case, he had taken carpenter's tools such as a saw and a plane; in your mother's case, such small items as a shawl, a pair of boots and an umbrella. They were not, I am afraid, first offenders. Both of them had been in prison before in Scotland, no doubt for similar offences. The witness at their marriage, Ann Lewis, was likewise transported for petty larceny. Her husband however, Robert Somerville Playfair, was a more unusual case. (I confess these early convict records hold a strange fascination for me!) His crime was forgery, a very serious offence as you will know, and he had completed a full sentence of ten years' hard labour in the colony. I have discovered no further details but would be willing to pursue the matter should you wish it. I trust that this information will cause you no pain or embarrassment. Your late parents had paid the full penalty for their misdemeanours and were free to put the memory of their convict days behind them. I trust that they did so. I have often heard it said that the Reverend H. P. Fry took a particular pleasure in joining in holy wedlock those couples who were convicts or who had once been convicts. He frequently said that nothing but good could come from it.

I remain,

Yours faithfully,

James Langtree, Curate, St George's Church, Hobart.

"Convicts!" gasped Mr Mallorie. "Both of them! Convicts!"

He took the letter from me and read it over to himself, very slowly.

"A saw and a plane," he murmured, "a shawl and boots and an umbrella! But, lass!" He looked up at me. "Me mother was a blinking saint! I knew her through and through! She

143

loved them old songs — and them old Psalms! How could she steal an umbrella?"

He had tears in his eyes.

I thought fast. I talked fast.

"You mustn't worry about it, Mr Mallorie," I said. "She only took a few little things. She must've been terribly poor. Hungry and poor. She wasn't wicked. You know that. You really knew her."

"Your mother knew her too, lass, when she was a girl."

"Yes. And she's often told me what a good mother she was to you. And what a wonderful son you were to your mother, too."

"Does she say that? Your mother says that?"

I nodded.

"We won't never tell her, lass. We won't tell no one about this letter. I don't want no one in the whole world to know. If yer Dad asks me again, I'll just say he was right all along. 'Free settler', I'll say to him. 'That must be it,' I'll say. You won't tell him, lass? You won't let on? You won't tell your Dad or your Mother, will you?"

"Never!" I said. And I never did.

We were silent for a while. Mr Mallorie rubbed his old eyes with the back of his hand.

"Forgery!" I said at last. "What exactly is it, Mr Mallorie?"

"I think it's copying someone else's signature like. To get money that isn't rightly yours. Or it could be printing bad money. Bank notes. That's forgery too. Playfair was a printer, don't forget."

"Will we tell her?"

"Tell who? Tell what?" he said.

"Miss Playfair. The Schoolie. Tell her that her grandfather was a forger."

"No, lass! Don't tell her! Whatever you do, don't tell!"

"Why not?"

"There's her Dad to think of, lass. There's that young Col Douglas she's going to marry. There's Mr and Mrs Douglas too. Miss Playfair's going to live her whole life here at Deepwater. She couldn't never hold her head up if you told her about her Grandpa."

"Are forgers clever, Mr Mallorie?" I asked.

"Very clever. No wonder her Dad's so smart. He's got that good job in the railways. Not jist driving trains, neither. She's pretty clever herself. Look at that Pageant she put on before Christmas. That was clever, I reckon."

"Couldn't I just tell Dad?" I suggested.

"No! Don't you tell no one, lass. That Miss Playfair has a few things to learn in life but it's not for us to teach her. Life'll teach her."

I was disappointed. I'm ashamed to admit it now but there was something in me that wanted to hurt Miss Playfair. She needed to be taken down a peg or two I thought. As I'd read that curate's letter, I'd even begun to wonder if she'd somehow already suspected that her grandfather had been a convict. She might have guessed the meaning of 'Free' and guessed it right. She'd be sure to want to keep it dark. I wanted to blurt it out. But I saw the sense of what Mr Mallorie had said. Anyway I could hardly blab about Grandpa Playfair without blabbing about nice old Mrs Mallorie at the same time. Those two secrets were tied together. I couldn't undo the knot without hurting Mr Mallorie himself. He was shattered by his discovery but so long as no one else knew it — apart from me — he could begin to forget.

"All right," I said. "I won't tell her. And I won't tell Dad. I won't breathe a word. Not for seventy years!"

He laughed.

"Seventy years! That'll be safe enough. No one won't ever be bothered about convicts in seventy years. In fact some people might even be proud of their convicts in seventy years."

Slowly he folded the letter in two. He ripped it across and then across again. I reached out and helped him. We tore that letter into tiny shreds and threw the bits onto the fire in his stove. Miss Playfair's grandfather was safe. And Mr Mallorie could go on thinking of his mother as a saint.

"She loved all them old Psalms, lass," he called after me as I left him to walk down the hill to our farmhouse. "Did I ever tell you that? She loved all them old Psalms."

12. *Gallipoli*

On 25th April, 1915, the Australian and New Zealand troops
landed in the dark of early morning on the tip of the Gallipoli
Peninsula. They climbed up the steep cliffs and into the
gullies. Anzac Cove, they called that landing place. Over the
next fifty years and longer we were to hear about those
Gallipoli landings again and again. The children heard of
Gallipoli in their schools; congregations heard of it in church;
old soldiers recalled it at thousands of Anzac Day Parades up
and down the whole country. And not just the landings
themselves. We were also to hear about the terrible battles
with the Turks that came afterwards. The battles at Bloody
Angle, at Courtney's Post, at Steele's Post, at the Knife Edge,
at Quinn's Post and at Lone Pine. All those names were to
become familiar to us over the years.

The strange thing was that at the time, in April 1915, we
heard very little news at all. We had no idea in the days after
the 25th that anything had happened over there. As far as we
knew, the boys were still in Egypt waiting for orders. There
was no radio in those days. We had to wait for Miss Playfair's
Argus to arrive from Melbourne. Not one word of Gallipoli was
reported till the issue of April 30 and that didn't reach
Deepwater till the first week of May. Even then, it told us very
little.

AUSTRALIANS IN ACTION
FIGHTING AGAINST TURKS
SPLENDID GALLANTRY SHOWN

There were no more details in the paper so we just had to
make them up. We imagined a tremendous victory with the
Turks swept away before our gallant boys. We were wildly

excited in the kitchen that afternoon as we read those headlines over and over again. Mr Douglas arrived on horseback waving his newspaper in the air. He was having the *Argus* sent up from the city too.

"They'll all be there, Alec!" he cried. "My Col and young Ronnie; your Laurie, the Craik boys and the Henschkes. They're heroes! Every one of them's a hero. They'll chase those Turks into the sea!"

"They're in the thick of it all right, Frank," said Dad proudly.

"It won't be long now," said Miss Playfair. "Then it will all be over."

She was more than excited. She was ecstatic. This was the glorious hour she had dreamed of. The turning of the tide, she called it. She was going to have those children in the school singing songs of victory all day long, she said.

"I hope you're right," said Mother. "About the turning of the tide."

Mr Douglas sat on with us in the kitchen for an hour or so that afternoon. Everyone was late with the evening milking. We passed the two identical newspapers from hand to hand. Mr Mallorie was there at the table. He was almost as excited as the rest of us. Mother poured tea. Bernie came running in. He'd just heard the news at the store and dashed straight up to tell us in case we hadn't heard. He sat down beside me, his fair face bright with excitement and his blue eyes shining.

"I do hope Laurie'll be all right," said Mother, breaking in on the jubilation.

"Of course he'll be all right, Em," said Dad. "He's a sensible boy."

"All our boys are sensible," she answered, "but that doesn't make them bullet-proof."

I shuddered at that word 'bullet'. It was something cold and hard that I never wanted to think about.

"Don't you worry, Mrs Ross," beamed Mr Douglas.

"Our prayers can help them," said Miss Playfair.

"Hmph!" said Mr Mallorie and sipped his hot tea noisily.

"Fred prays for Martin and Hans every night," said Bernie,

grinning at me, "but he's afraid God mightn't know their new names!"

Everyone laughed. Even Mother.

"Listen!" said Dad suddenly. "What's that?"

We listened. We all looked up at the ceiling. We rushed to the window. We ran out of the back door. The unbelievable miracle had begun! It was raining!

First the rain came in slow heavy drops. They bounced noisily off the iron roof. Then it fell in a steady drenching downpour. Finally it came in thick white sheets of water that unrolled endlessly from the sky. Day after day it went on falling, night after night. The long drought had broken at last.

Even Miss Playfair ran with us into the rain as the first drops fell. She didn't really like to get wet but she got a proper soaking that day. Her long dripping skirt clung to her legs. Mr Douglas and Dad leaped about like school boys. Bernie and I ran down to the Henschkes' farm. He took my hand as we ran. I was surprised by that but I liked it. Down there the whole family was standing out in the rain and letting it soak into them. The ruined garden, now well on the mend, was awash. I hugged Ruth. She was laughing and smiling like the old Ruth I used to know. I hugged her again.

The rest of that day has faded from me now into a happy hazy memory. I don't recall what else we did or what we said or when I trudged back home again after dark. All I can remember is that hours later I was lying in bed, listening to the beautiful thunder of rain on our roof. I was singing at the top of my voice. No one could possibly hear me. The rain was far too loud. And while I sang so lustily I also cried. No one could hear that either. I don't know why I cried. I've often wondered.

Miss Playfair was wrong about Gallipoli. It wasn't really a turning of the tide at all. The worst battles still lay ahead of the troops and when they happened we heard hardly a word about them. The triumphant headlines went on through June and July.

THRILLING EXPERIENCE
A BONZER GO

HEROISM OF OUR GUNNERS
MEN IN SPLENDID SPIRITS
GALLANT DEEDS OF SOLDIERS

We heard nothing of the terrible slaughter at the time. We thought it was a famous victory.

But the ending of the drought was a turning of the tide all right. Our river was running deep again and overflowing its banks within hours. All the little creeks were gurgling and splashing down from the ridge. The dry dams filled with water. Gillespie's Track was almost a river itself! The scraggy cows and sheep stood bewildered in their sodden paddocks and huddled under the trees for protection. The rain didn't stop for ten days. On and on. Our troubles were over.

But not quite. It was in May and June and July that the first dreaded telegrams began to arrive in the valley. Black-edged for a death. Plain-edged for a wound. They weren't just left to be collected at the little local post-offices. They were delivered right to the farmhouse door by special messengers on horse or even on bicycle. Mother used to stand out on our front verandah, looking along the Track, hoping against hope that she'd see no messenger coming on his way to our farm.

He didn't ever come to our farm but he went to the Henschkes. Hans was dead on Gallipoli. Henry Henderson — as the telegram said. Bernie brought us the terrible news and we all rode down to the Henschkes' at once. There was Mrs Henschke, still standing on her verandah, the telegram still in her hand. It seemed as if she could not move.

"Emily!" she cried as we ran in through the gate. That was the only time I ever heard her use Mother's first name. Her voice was wooden and strange. "It's come, Emily! It's come!"

She fell into Mother's arms. They went in together to the parlour. Mother shut the door but I didn't want to follow. That would have been too terrible. Bernie and Dad and I went into the kitchen. All the family was there, ranged around the long table, with Mr Henschke at the head. Fred and Lisa and Kate had red swollen eyes. The two little ones hardly seemed to realize what had happened. Margaret, the nearest to Hans in age, sat white and silent. Ruth was holding her arm and talking to her. Everyone moved up and they brought more chairs so we could sit too. I was between Ruth and Bernie, just the way we'd always been at school all those years.

To my amazement Mr Henschke was pouring glasses of last year's wine for all of us. Even for Harry and Tom though theirs were topped up with water.

"Hans is dead," he said slowly.

I wondered why he had to be so brutal — to spell it out so bluntly. We all knew Hans was dead. Why couldn't he keep quiet about it now?

"Hans was only eighteen," he went on. "We can't have a funeral. He'll be buried on Gallipoli in a grave we'll never see. But if we were able to have a funeral, when it was all over we'd come back here to the house and we'd sit around this table with the wine and we'd talk about Hans. We'd remember all those things we loved about him. We'd tell each other about the funny things he used to do. And that's what we're going to do now."

"No, Dad!" protested Margaret. "I don't want to remember. It hurts too much. I just can't take it in. I don't believe Hans is dead. It can't be true!"

Mr Henschke was very gentle with her.

"It *is* true, Margie," he said. "You saw the telegram. That's why I want us to remember. I'm going to tell you about the night Hans was born. It was here in this house, of course, where all of you were born. We'd sent for the doctor but he came far too late. I was the one who helped Hans into the world."

I was rather embarrassed. I didn't want to hear all about Hans's birth just when we were thinking about his death. But Mr Henschke went on. I didn't know much about birth in those days. And Mr Henschke didn't actually tell us what it was really like though he'd been there to see it all. I was glad he didn't. What he did tell us was about the baby itself — its funny bald head, its clear blue eyes, its wailing cry. And he told us about Martin and Margaret coming in to see the baby.

"I think we could send it back now, Dad," Martin had said

when he'd had a good long look.

We all laughed. That broke the ice. The memories came flooding thick and fast. Memories of Hans. Margaret had the most to tell. She'd known him the longest. But even the two little ones had their stories. And I did too. The day Hans had tied my plaits to the back of the chair at school. The day, years before, when he'd tried to teach me to ride a horse when I was still only three and he was seven.

That was a strange afternoon in the Henschkes' kitchen. I've never forgotten it. The death of Hans was the first death that really touched me. My Grandpa had died when I was about ten and I'd been sad, naturally. But he was old and he'd had a good life. He was ready to go. Hans wasn't old. He was only a boy. He was one of us at Deepwater. Would he ever have gone to the war if it hadn't been for Miss Playfair and her white feathers? Was she to blame? I've often wondered. And over the years, as new deaths have come to me, each one brings back with a sudden unexpected quirk of memory that death of Hans Henschke in 1915. Whenever I cry for another death I cry for Hans again too. I'm glad we sat round the table and told those stories. It was the best funeral I've ever been to. The best and the worst.

The Henschkes weren't the only family to get a telegram. The Douglases had two late in June. One came one day and one the next. Ronnie Douglas was dead. Col was wounded. We just couldn't believe it. Miss Playfair couldn't believe it.

"He's only twenty-two!" she kept saying over and over again.

I don't know why she said that. Ronnie was the one that was dead and he was only twenty. Age had nothing to do with it.

The Douglases were stunned. They made Stu promise that he'd never ever go to the war, not if it lasted for fifty years. He promised all right. He'd seen what war could do. Now all the thoughts of the family were turned to Col. What was his wound, they asked each other many times a day? Was it serious or not? Where exactly was he now? Would he come home? Miss Playfair constantly asked us the very same questions whenever she was with us. We had no answers. Sometimes she wasn't with us at all. She went more and more often to the Douglases' house. Sometimes she stayed the night. Their grief drew them together. Grief and fear. They heard no more news of Col for weeks.

When at last a letter came, the news was good. Or quite good. Col couldn't write himself but he'd asked his mate to write for him. He said he was fine. He could walk and talk, he said. Don't worry, he said.

Then they heard Col was coming home. On a troop ship that was sailing to Australia to collect more soldiers for the war. Mr Mallorie was gloomy about this.

"He must be bad," he said to us. I was glad Miss Playfair wasn't there to hear him. "When the wounds aren't too deep, they patch them up quick and send them back to the front line. If he's coming home, he must be bad."

"He probably can't hold the gun," said Mother. "He might've been wounded in the arms. It's not his legs. He says he can walk. If you can't hold the gun, you can't be a soldier, can you?"

"He'll be home by the end of September, Frank Douglas says," said Dad. "Then we'll all know."

When the school holiday came round late in August, Miss Playfair didn't go down to the city. She moved all her things to the Douglases' house. She wanted to be there for Col's great homecoming and they were glad to have her.

Mr Douglas said he'd have the Wallaceville town band at the railway station to greet Col. I thought he was just joking but he meant it. The band was there on the day. I was there too. So was everyone from Deepwater. In fact all the families from the valley were there at the station to welcome Col Douglas back to Gillespie's Track.

I stood with Dad and Mother and all the Henschkes. Well in front of us, near the edge of the platform, were the Douglases — Stu and Phyllis, Ken and Norm, Grace and Bob. Miss Playfair herself stood between Mr and Mrs Douglas, their eyes fixed on the railway line that came from the south. Around them were the Logans and the Morisons and the

Pollocks from the store. The train roared in. The band began to play. We all stood waiting for Col to appear.

Two young soldiers in khaki uniforms stepped briskly out of the train. Each of them wore a red cross on a broad white arm band. We stared at them blankly. We'd never seen either of them before. They weren't from our valley. The two soldiers turned back to the carriage door and put up their big hands to help the next man down. He stood there, framed in the doorway, supported by one soldier on each side. It was Col. His legs were all right — just as he'd said. But one of his arms had gone. The empty sleeve was turned up and pinned to his shoulder. And a thick white bandage was wrapped round and round his eyes. He couldn't see! Col Douglas was blind!

"Colin!" shrieked Miss Playfair and ran towards him. She flung her arms around him and buried her face in his khaki coat. Mr Douglas held up his hand.

"Stop!" he called. And the band stopped playing.

So Miss Playfair lived on in our valley for the rest of her life. Mrs Douglas, I mean. It was never an easy marriage. Col Douglas was a hard man. His blindness made him harder. I can understand that. He couldn't or wouldn't work on the farm. He just sat about on the verandah, grumbling and sniping. But I never heard Miss Playfair complain. Not once in all those years. She was always a lady, Mother used to say. She didn't teach any more. Married women weren't allowed to teach in those days. She stayed at home and helped Mrs Douglas in the kitchen. She never had any children. When old Mr Douglas died, Col's young brothers, Stu and Ken took over the running of the farm. Their sons and their grandsons are still running it today. It's a good farm.

As for me, four years later, when the war was well over, I married Bernie Henschke. Does that surprise you? It surprised me! I never thought I'd end up as a farmer's wife by Gillespie's Track. I never thought I'd want to live out my whole long life at Deepwater. But Mother always said she wasn't surprised at all. She could see it coming a mile off! That's what she used to say.

The Henschke puppets came out of hiding on our wedding

day. I'd almost forgotten what they looked like but the paint hadn't faded at all. Mr Henschke set up his little theatre on our front verandah and made his puppets leap about the stage. Kasper was there and the Grandma; Gretchen and the Wicked Robber. All the families from Deepwater and Kanyul gathered round to see them dancing together and to hear the old familiar lines. The Wicked Robber repented and Kasper married his Gretchen. The Grandmother smiled and sang in her high squeaky voice that I remembered so well from the years before the war. The German Bible came out of hiding too and Mr Henschke wrote my name beside Bernie's on the page for family marriages.

Mrs Henschke wore black on the day of our wedding though she was happy for Bernie and me. She wore black for the rest of her life. In memory of Hans. No one blamed her for that — even on a wedding day. How could she ever forget?

I wore the creamy white satin dress that Mother had worn on her own wedding day. It fitted me well. Mother dabbed my face with powder just before we set off for the church to try to make me look less brown and sunburnt. The white powder rubbed off in patches as the warm day wore on. Ruth was my bridesmaid, of course. She was to be the next girl in our valley to marry — but that's another story.

Mr Mallorie gave us his stone as a present. A present for Bernie and me. He slipped it into Bernie's pocket on the day of the wedding and told him he'd like us to keep it. I don't know why he did that. I thought he was going to leave it to Miss Playfair — Mrs Douglas, I mean — when he finally wrote out his will. He must have changed his mind. It's true she never seemed to want it. Bernie was fond of that stone. The stone from a beach in Tasmania. He threaded a strong piece of string through the hole and he hung it up over our door. Summer and winter it swings in the wind but the pebble has not fallen out.